My Friend Mothman

By
Lauren Devora

Acknowledgements

For Brigid, for all that you've done.

For my family, both blood and chosen.

For the enduring people of
Point Pleasant, West Virginia.

Thank you.

Thank you.

Thank you.

And Mothman, if you're reading this, thank you for lending your image and inspiration.

I hope I did you justice.

Copyright © 2020 by Lauren Devora

All rights reserved. No part of this book may be reproduced in any form on by an electronic or mechanical means, including information storage and retrieval systems, without permission in writing from the publisher, except by a reviewer who may quote brief passages in a review.

Chapter One

Wendy heard him before she saw him.

Over the hum of voices filling the Ohio State student union, she recognized the squeak of converse sneakers and displeased grunting.

She tracked his approach, bracing for impact.

Three... Two...

In a flurry of plaid and denim, Victor dropped into his chair, muttering as he logged into the university computer.

"I can't believe Doctor Bledsoe won't let me take my proposal to the department head." The table rattled as he kicked his bookbag underneath. "I mean, I already did the heavy lifting. All they have to do is sign off on it."

Wendy sighed, gaze flicking up from the article she was proof reading for the school paper.

"Vic, you want the anthropology department and the biology department to create a new major for you." She waited for him to look over the edge of his computer monitor. "That's ludicrous."

He pushed a few rouge chocolate brown locks off his forehead. "You sound just like Doctor B."

"Not just any major, a major about something that doesn't exist."

"Hey now, don't kick a man while he's down."

Wendy rolled her eyes. "Cryptozoological anthropology can't be a major because the things you want to study can't be studied. You can't measure them, read up on their cultures, or ask them questions." She settled back into her chair, rereading the last paragraph of the piece. "Just be an Anthro major and study the myths and lore."

"You are such a buzzkill, you know that?" Victor said, leaning forward on his elbows.

"So I've been told."

Sweeping her thick blonde curls over her shoulder, Wendy squinted at an incorrect verb usage and reached for her pen.

A surprised gasp made her jerk, knocking her Bic to the floor.

"Ugh, Victor…"

"Sorry, sorry, I just…" He trailed off, nose centimeters from the screen. "Oh my God, they spotted him."

Making a pincher move with her fingers, she leaned over. "Spotted who?" Wendy asked, angling her neck as she reached down.

He smirked. "What do you care? You don't think they exist."

"Oh, shut up you big baby," she said, giving up her crab claw action and ducking under the table. "I can't believe you're on those monster sites while you're supposed to be writing a thousand words on the latest campus political rally."

"It's called self-care, Wendy," Victor stated. "I needed a few minutes with my babies, reminding myself what I'm fighting for."

Slowly crawling backwards, pen successfully in hand, Wendy scowled. "One, don't call them your 'babies'. And two, you're not a martyr for a cause. You're a conspiracy nut."

"Tell that to Mothman."

Wendy jumped, smacking the back of her head on the table corner.

Cursing under her breath, she scrambled to her feet. "What?"

"Once I get this major approved, all these cryptids will have the respect of the university and even the public. Oh my god, can you imagine if I get to speak at a convention? I'll be the next—"

"What is that?" Wendy swayed, rubbing her head as she bent over Victor's shoulder to stare at the computer screen.

"I told you," Victor said, looking up at her. "It's a photo of Mothman. A really good one too. I mean, look at that resolution."

"That's..." She blinked.

It couldn't be.

It looked like him... The massive dark wings were a huge giveaway.

But... It couldn't be him...

She recognized the buildings, but not because they were in her hometown.

The skyline looked like Pittsburgh.

"Victor, when was this taken?"

"This morning. Crypto-watchers keep on the ball with their posts, to maintain the accuracy of the timeline."

Wendy's stomach dropped.

What was he doing in Pennsylvania?

"Pretty cool, huh?" Victor glanced up at her again, smiling.

Taking a step back, she nodded once before rushing to her bookbag, shoving her stuff inside as quickly as she could.

"Vic, take over for me," she said, slinging her bag over her shoulder. "I have to go."

"Take over?" Victor swiveled his chair, staring after her. "But you're the editor. Wendy!"

She was already halfway to the door, dodging around clusters of people.

Sophomores were allowed cars on campus, a huge plus for an out of state student, but in that moment, she was just thankful she'd parked close.

The drive from Ohio State University back to Point Pleasant was nearly a straight shot, but those two hours behind the wheel had never felt longer in Wendy's life.

As the sun set, her anxiety tripled until she felt sick to her stomach.

Why would he leave? He'd never gone farther than campus that *one* time, and that was off-the-charts risky. What would make him go all the way to Pittsburgh?

Pulling off Potters Creek Road, she parked her beat up two-door Honda on the first flat patch of ground she could, and jumped out, flashlight and phone in hand.

Taking off at a jog, careful to avoid any stumps or gopher holes, she followed the path she'd had memorized since she was a little girl.

Greyish pink dusk turned into night just as she saw the door to the ammunitions igloo—a large concrete structure covered by mounds of soil and moss, surrounded by trees.

"Greg!" She slowed her pace, trying to catch her breath. "Greg, where are you?"

Shuffling—quiet, unsure footsteps—sounded from inside. Wendy clicked her flashlight on, sweeping the beam over the ground towards the heavy steel door.

The hinges groaned as it opened, revealing only pitch darkness.

"Greg?"

Two red eyes appeared near the top of the doorframe, glowing like reflectors on a pedal bike.

Wendy exhaled fully, relief flooding her system.

A shadow split away from the darkness inside the bunker, emerging into the clearing to stand at his full height. Shaking his wings out, he chirped at her in confusion.

"Did you leave?" Wendy asked, stepping closer. "This morning? Yesterday?"

He furrowed his brow, shaking his head. *"No,"* he clicked.

"You didn't go to Pittsburgh?"

Another set of rapid clicks. *"Why would I go to Pittsburgh?"*

Turning her flashlight off, Wendy said, "Well, that's what I drove all the way out here to find out. I thought you'd..."

Understanding hit her harder than her eight-a.m. coffee order.

"Greg, someone took a picture this morning…" She started, crossing the small clearing. "It looked just like you."

"I promise I didn't—"

"I know, I know." She arched her neck to look up at him. "But if that picture wasn't of you, that means…" Wendy swallowed. "Greg, I think there are more of you. I think there are more Mothmen."

* * * * * * *

June 12th, 2007

Point Pleasant, West Virginia

Wendy finished tying her braids with her favorite green hairbands as she wandered into the kitchen. The sounds of a NASCAR race rumbled from the TV set in the living room. Clearly her daddy had already figured out his day plans.

"Mama, can I go to Rebecca's to play?"

Darlene turned, blonde curls bouncing around her face.

Wendy loved her mother's hair. Loved it because it matched her own. It was confirmation that they had at least one thing in common.

"Oh, honey, I don't know…" *Darlene frowned at the clock.* "I'd have to drive you and I'm already late for my shift at the diner."

"I can walk," Wendy exclaimed, certain her enthusiasm would be the selling point.

"No sugar, you can't walk all the way there, it's too far."

"I can ride my bike."

"I meant, it's too far for you to walk unsupervised," her mother corrected, gathering up her bag and keys. *"Just stay here with your daddy today and then maybe tomorrow you can go play with Rebecca, okay?"*

Disappointment pinched Wendy's features. "Okay."

Smiling, Darlene bent down to kiss her on the forehead. "Have a good day. Be good," she said as she left out the backdoor.

Wendy sighed. Opening the fridge to grab a juice box, she made her way into the living room, absolutely, one hundred percent pouting.

"Hey, sport," John called, barely moving from his preferred lounging position on the couch. *"What you up to today?"*

Punching the straw through the foil circle, Wendy shrugged. "Wanted to go to Rebecca's…"

Scratching his chest through his shirt, he watched her for a moment.

"Oh yeah? What'd your mama say?"

"She said maybe tomorrow."

John looked from Wendy to the bright sunny day showcased by the big window in their living room and then back again.

His resolve was never firm to begin with when it came to Wendy, but she could tell it was crumbling with every whir of the ceiling fan.

"Tomorrow, huh?" He glanced at the TV, watching the cars circle the track. "Rebecca's ain't far, is it?"

Wendy shook her head, sucking down apple juice.

"You know the way?"

Wendy nodded.

Digging into his pocket, John took out his old Nokia prepaid and a ten-dollar bill. "You promise not to get into trouble?" He asked with a wink.

Wendy smiled, straw still clenched between her teeth.

"Here," he said, handing her the phone and cash. "Use that to call home if there's an emergency. And don't spend all that in one place."

Jumping up with her supplies and granted freedom, Wendy barreled towards the back door.

"Be careful now!" John called. "Don't go messin' where you shouldn't and be home before your mama gets back!"

"Bye, daddy! Love you!" She answered, shoving the blocky phone and folded bill into the pocket of her Wal-Mart Kids cargo green shorts.

Wendy hated summer. It was too hot, too humid, and the amount of mosquito bites she found on her arms and legs doubled by the day.

But summer meant long days with plenty of sunlight, and a free schedule to be filled with exploring. Trips to the pond behind grandpa's house to look for tadpoles. Long walks through McClintic reserve. July Fourth brought fireworks and cook-outs and lots of swimming.

Pedaling to the end of her street, Wendy looked both ways before crossing, braids bumping against her bare shoulders, tickling her. She adjusted the strap of her new tank top—white and green stripes with a giraffe on the front.

Giraffes had been her favorite since the day she'd learned about them. Long goofy necks and wide purple tongues they used to pull leaves off branches. She thought they were just about the weirdest creature she'd ever seen, and she loved them.

Making a left, Wendy biked by houses she recognized from the drive to school. Rebecca didn't live that far on the other side of the elementary school, in a blue house with yellow shutters and a flag outside.

She kept looking for the flag, knew it had to be close...

Dread—the kind that filled her stomach like bad pasta salad—started to take hold as Wendy glanced around.

She must've missed the turn.

Looping the block, she hoped she'd remember it from the other direction, but still there was no blue house, no yellow shutters, no flag.

Puffing her cheeks out like a blowfish, she went back, deciding to keep biking the direction she'd been going.

Maybe if she got out of that neighborhood, she'd find the right road.

Minutes passed. The houses got smaller and farther apart. Then the pavement turned to gravel.

Wendy was lost.

She started to take out her dad's cellphone, defeat and embarrassment burning her cheeks worse than the noonday sun.

In the distance, a broken fence caught her attention, and Wendy left the phone in her pocket.

A smile creeped across her face.

Her favorite books always started with someone getting lost in a deep, dark forest. The opportunity to have her own adventure was just too good to pass up.

Setting her bike down in the weeds, she walked over, dragging her hand against the rusted chain link with a brrrump, brrrump, brrrump.

One faded sign read 'No Trespassing', right next to a gaping hole in the fence where someone else had ignored that warning.

Well, if they could do it…

She glanced over her shoulder at the vast emptiness of the field around her.

Now or never.

Wendy ducked, wriggling through, careful not to tear any of her clothes. Her mama would kill her if she ripped her new shorts.

The unkempt acreage made her feel like she was on safari in Africa, searching for lions or elephants.

Or giraffes.

It was a little itchy though.

Picking up a stick, Wendy swung it through the grass, watching grasshoppers leap away from the danger.

After a minute of trudging, and only tripping once, she spotted an abandoned building surrounded by thin saplings. The outer concrete walls were cracked and crumbling, with kudzu vines climbing all the way to the decaying roof. Most of the windows were busted out, either with baseball sized holes in the panes or missing them entirely.

So, this was the thing worth keeping people away from...

It was like a creepy fortress in one of the many fairytales she'd read, left just for her to find.

Glass and pebbles crunched under her sneakers as she walked up to the front, bending back to stare all the way to the top.

"Wow," she whispered, stepping inside.

The second and third floors had all fallen away, leaving steel beams crisscrossing above her, and concrete pillars holding the structure in place.

It was infinitely cooler inside, shaded by the remainder of the metal roof, and she wiped the sweat off the back of her neck as she looked around.

To the left, a pile of rubble sat just tall enough to climb up to reach the first section of beams. With a grin, Wendy discarded her stick and started crawling.

Halfway up, her foot slid in the loose gravel and she gasped. Finding her grip on a piece of rebar, she held herself in place and let out an exhilarated giggle, continuing her trek.

From behind her, a heavy chunk of concrete rolled across the foundation below.

"Hello?" She called, twisting to look.

Nothing.

Spine prickling with fear, Wendy considered her options. She could head back down, run for her bike...

But none of the heroes of her stories would run. So, neither would she.

Hurrying her way up to the beam, she swung her leg over so she could straddle it.

From her perch, she scanned the building.

She was higher than she thought... Much higher.

Pushing onto her hands and knees, Wendy steadied herself and stood up like she'd done once before at gymnastics camp. Arms out for balance, she put one foot in front of the other, toe to heel, walking across the beam with ease.

A pillar blocked her path across the rest of the beam, and she turned slowly, slowly, slowly around, keeping her balance. She'd have to go back the way she came.

From the corner of her eye she saw a shadow peel away from another pillar. Before she could focus, the giant black form darted across the second floor supports, gusts of air swirling behind it.

Wendy screamed, her foot slipping over the edge. Arms flailing, she flapped wildly to regain her balance, but it was too late. She tipped, soles of her worn out sneakers dragging helplessly against concrete.

The ground below came into hyper-focus.

She was falling...

Until she wasn't.

Something had her by the hand, keeping her suspended in the air.

Dangling only a few feet below the beam she'd been standing on, Wendy kicked her feet instinctively.

Terrified, barely breathing, she glanced from the floor to her limp shoelaces and then upwards.

Someone had caught her.

*Some **thing**.*

A shadow. A shadow with arms. Long fingers that hurt the back of her wrist—talons pressing into her skin.

Huge black wings blocked out the light, face indistinguishable from the rest of him.

But she saw eyes.

Bright, glowing red eyes that were too wide and round for a human.

Before Wendy could scream, the shadow was pulling her up until they were nose to nose.

*So he **did** have a nose...*

Tilting his head, he watched her a moment, before setting her down gently on her feet. He didn't let go, seemingly aware of her inability to keep her legs sturdy beneath her, but his grip loosened.

Wendy finally took a deep breath.

She blinked, staring up to take in his full, monstrous height.

"I... I..." She licked her dry lips. "I don't know how to get down."

The creature glanced from her to the ground below.

Crouching, he offered her his hand, if it could be called that, and waited.

Wendy thought for a beat, considering her other alternatives.

It could be a trap, but he hadn't let her fall before...

Taking his hand, she let him pick her up, scooping her into his arms just like her daddy would to take her to bed when she'd fallen asleep on the sofa. Extending his wings, he glided down off the beam with ease.

Landing with a soft thud, he set her down in a patch of sunlight near the door.

Wendy wanted to run. Could've jumped up fast, scrambled out of the building, and tore through the grass back to her bike, back to her home, never to set foot there again.

She dug her heel into the dirt, ready to do just that.

Then she saw his face—finally able to make out the angles and planes of his features in the light. It was the sag of his eyebrows that made her pause.

In that moment, he looked like the loneliest being on the planet.

Wendy knew about the monster said to live around Point Pleasant. Had heard her daddy and grandpa whispering stories, some new, some old. Her mama never gave them much mind, always saying it was just a big bird or a trick played by tired eyes on fearful minds.

People said he was evil. Terrifying. An omen.

But the giant shadow kneeling in front of her didn't seem so bad. And he did save her life…

Distress ebbed from her body, leaving a wake of renewed confidence.

Sitting up straighter, Wendy stuck out her hand like grown ups did when they met someone new.

"Hi. My name's Wendy," she said. "What's yours?"

The creature looked at her hand and flexed his own, unsure of the custom.

"Don't you have a name?"

Big red eyes blinked at her. Then he shook his head.

"Oh," she said, letting her hand drop. "Well, everybody should have a name." Poking at the dirt by her shoe, she thought it over. "Can you talk?"

He chirped, high and short like a bird. Wendy giggled at the sound.

"That's not talking," she said, still smiling. "Not like me anyway. But I guess it's talking like you."

Folding his wings against his back, he sat across from her, one abnormally long leg bent close to his chest.

"Hmm... You don't look like anything else I've seen, so I don't know what to call you." *She looked up at him, taking in the details of his face. He was more humanoid than people had said.* "What about Michael?"

The creature made a guttural noise, trying to replicate the name. It sounded nothing like Michael.

Wendy laughed, shaking her head. "Nope. How about Chris?"

He tried again, hissing.

After attempting the few boy names she could remember, Wendy was about to give up when she thought of one she hadn't heard in a while.

"Hey, what about Greg?"

The creature lifted an eyebrow in interest and opened his mouth. **"Gurg."**

"That was pretty close. Try again?"

"Gurg."

Wendy shrugged. "Guess that'll have to do." *Sticking her hand out again, she said,* "Nice to meet you, Greg."

That time he figured out what to do.

Chapter Two

Wendy paced back and forth in a tight loop. "Okay, so if that picture wasn't of you—"

"I told you it wasn't," he chirped, watching her from his perch in a nearby tree.

"I know, I'm sorry," she said, chewing the corner of her thumbnail. "I believe you, Greg. I do. I just…" She stopped mid-stride. "Greg, do you know what this means?"

He waited.

"It means you're not alone," she said, looking up at him. "All these years, and… And you have family out there."

His clicks were sharper than usual. Greg was irritated. *"You don't know that for sure. It was just one picture. Besides, I have family **here**."*

His last point was a punch to Wendy's gut. "Oh, Greg, I didn't mean…" She shook her head. "I just know what it's been like for you."

She stared up at him in the dark. Red eyes amidst the inky black shape of him—head barely distinguishable from the curve of his folded wings, massive frame looming in the branches.

Greg was special, not just to her but to the town. For decades, Point Pleasant had claimed him as their own cryptid. A supernatural mascot of sorts.

And now, she might have stumbled upon proof that Greg wasn't the only one of his kind. Proof he wasn't alone in the world.

But that would also mean he didn't belong to them anymore.

"We don't have to go looking. We can forget it if you want." She sighed. "But Greg, don't you want to know if there are others? Aren't you curious?"

The curve of his wings shifted—the only clue in the dark that he was shrugging—before he clicked and grunted. *"You think the picture was real?"*

Wendy nodded. "If it wasn't, it was a damn good fake."

Leaves rustled in a soft breeze as the quiet stretched between them.

She'd always wondered what the future would hold for Greg. Knew she wouldn't be around forever, that life would take her away from Point Pleasant eventually, and that Greg would be right back to where he started.

Alone, with no one else around who knew for sure he even existed.

But maybe, just maybe, that wouldn't have to be the case after all.

Greg shifted in the tree, making an agreeable noise at the back of his throat.

"Maybe... There's no harm in finding out for sure."

* * * * * * *

June 14th, 2007

"How do you say 'apple'?"

Two clicks and a 'haa' sound. Wendy smiled.

"What about 'dog'?"

A low grunt.

"That sounds like when my daddy stubs his toe," she giggled. Picking up a smaller rock, Wendy chucked it into the creek. "Did you always know English, or did you have to learn?"

Greg crouched at her side, watching her pick which stones to toss. He chirped and shrugged.

"You don't remember?"

He shook his head, dark grey skin covered in light fuzz catching the morning light filtering through the leaves.

Wendy threw another rock, waiting for the splash before asking, "Why not?"

Greg glanced up at the clouds for a moment, thick brows furrowed. Gathering a small pebble between two claws, he showed it to Wendy before tossing it up into the air and watching it fall to the ground. He pointed to the rock and then himself.

"You... fell?"

Greg nodded. Tapping his temple with one talon, he gestured to the rock again before shaking his head.

"You hit your head?"

He clicked once—*A yes.*

Wendy frowned at the rock. "And that made you forget everything?"

Greg shrugged, chirping.

Wendy could decipher a little... Something about a long time ago and loss.

"I think I heard my mama talk about something like that," Wendy said. "Something called **am…tisia?**"

A wet hissing noise followed by a '**heh heh heh**' made her jolt.

Greg's thin dark lips were pulled back, exposing two rows of short, pointed teeth as his shoulders bounced.

"What?" Wendy smiled, feeling her ears burn. "Are you laughin' at me?"

He continued to chuckle, gurgling like he was talking under water. Finally, he nodded, and chirped at her.

"Fine, maybe that's not the word," she said, playfully tossing a handful of dirt at his giant clawed foot. "But I'll look it up later."

Finding a short stick, Wendy poked at the wet ground by the creek bed.

"I'm sorry you don't remember anything. That must've been really scary."

Greg clicked a few times and shrugged.

Dark hand clasping her shoulder gently, he waited for her to look up. Muddy-red eyes welled with emotion as he stared at her.

He didn't have to translate that time. Wendy could sense the meaning behind the gesture.

It was scary, but I managed. Thank you for caring.

"I guess this means you don't know if you have a mom and dad, huh?" She asked.

Greg shook his head.

"One of the girls in my class is adopted," Wendy said, dropping her stick. "She doesn't know her real mom and dad either. But she seems happy anyway."

Clicking a short response, Greg nodded.

Wendy frowned, trying to puzzle out what he said.

"You want to be adopted too?"

He paused, blinking in surprise.

The two were silent for a beat before Greg smiled again, exposing his fang-like teeth.

A short chirp, high like a songbird, was his answer.

"Yes."

* * * * * * *

Something wet dripped onto Wendy's cheek, startling her out of a vague dream.

Blinking, she swatted her face, wiping the dew away.

At least, she hoped it was dew...

Sunlight glimmered through the leaves, and Wendy smiled drowsily. She loved sunrise.

Oh no. Sunrise.

"Crap," she yelped, scrambling up from her spot at the base of the tree. "Crap, crap, crap. Greg!"

An alarmed, high-pitched screech was cut off by the shaking of branches and a colossal thud behind her.

"Oh my God," she gasped, rushing to where Greg had fallen. "I'm *so* sorry."

Pushing onto his hands and knees, Greg groaned and shook his head to clear it.

Sliding her hands under his armpits, she hoisted him off the ground. "What happened to using your wings, huh?" Wendy teased.

Greg glared down at her, clicking a retort. *"I don't recall making fun of you when you fell out of your loft bed. Twice."*

"That wasn't my fault. I was a very active sleeper."

Dusting his chest off, Greg snorted. *"Sure."*

Bending to gather up her keys and phone, she told him, "Greg, I got to run. I didn't mean to fall asleep here and I'm going to be late to my first class."

"Where did you park?"

"Near the road."

Stretching his wings out, Greg lifted an eyebrow at her. *"Need a lift?"*

Wendy grinned.

There were a lot of unusual perks to being best friends with Mothman, but speedier travel was probably her favorite.

The only downside was the havoc it wreaked on her hair. As if she needed her curls to be even bigger.

Held securely in Greg's arms, he flew with her through the woods. Trees and shrubs blurred into a soft hazy pallet of greens and browns as he carried her towards Potters Creek Road. Keeping a safe distance from any low hanging branches, he glided down gently. Gusts of air battered the sides of her face as he flapped his wings and landed on his feet.

"Thanks, Greg," she said, climbing out of his grasp.

Scanning the road and surrounding fields for any early risers taking a walk through the wildlife reserve, Wendy stepped quietly to the edge of the tree line.

"I think it's clear, but you should probably stay hidden just in case."

Greg clicked in agreement, and Wendy darted out towards her car. She was almost two yards away before stopping dead and turning back.

Pushing back through the trees, Wendy launched at Greg, hugging him.

"Bye, Greg," she said into the dark grey fuzz of his torso.

"Not bye, just later," he told her in a hushed, guttural string of noises.

Wendy nodded, releasing her hold on him. "Right. Just later." Smiling up at him she started back towards the road. "Stay out of trouble, okay?"

Dropping into a crouch, Greg saluted her with two fingers, making her laugh.

She'd taught him that.

Hurrying to start her car, Wendy still took a moment to stare up at the brightening sky, waiting. As soon as she saw the silhouette of wings and a torso rising above the treetops, she put the gear into reverse, and pulled away from the reserve.

Chapter Three

Scooting into her morning history class just before the door was closed was embarrassing but a miracle, especially given how fast she drove on the highway.

If her father had seen the speedometer, he'd have had a stroke.

Tiptoeing to her usual seat, she slid into the desk next to Victor.

"Rough night?" He whispered, pretending to be reading the white board.

"What? No, of course not." Wendy shook her head, forcing her gaze forward.

Glancing over, Victor subtly reached behind her, pulling something from her tangled ponytail.

"You sure about that?" He asked, holding a twig in front of her face with a smirk.

Snatching it out of his hand, Wendy refused to look him in the eye. "I don't want to talk about it."

Victor chuckled. "Okay, weirdo."

She didn't have any of the right notebooks for this class, but Wendy was excellent at improvising. Scribbling her notes in the back of her designated economics binder, she tried to focus.

A much more difficult task than she'd anticipated.

Every few minutes her thoughts would drift.

Moth*men*. Plural. She reckoned she shouldn't gender them preemptively but seeing as she wasn't sure what else to call them, it was the only word she could think of.

Other Mothmen… There were others. They looked just like Greg.

And they were close—Close enough to travel to look for… But if they were so close, why hadn't they tried to find Greg? Could they sense him? Shouldn't they be able to? What if they weren't as friendly as Greg? What if—

"Hey, Nervous Nancy," Victor whispered to her. "You're about to vibrate out of your desk."

"Huh?" Wendy jolted, flinging her pen over her shoulder in a high arc.

It clattered on another student's desk before rolling into the dark unknown.

With burning cheeks, she faced forward, hoping no one else noticed.

She really needed to stop holding pens while she was anxious.

"You should consider cutting back on the caffeine," Victor said, handing her his pencil. "You're too young to die of a heart attack."

"Mister Valentine, is there something you'd like to add to the lecture?" Their professor asked, folding her arms over her chest.

"Not at all, Doctor Adams. I was conferring with my classmate about one of my notes. She pointed out my mistake. Thank you," he added, looking at Wendy.

"You're welcome," Wendy said hurriedly, folding her hands in her lap.

Doctor Adams didn't look convinced, but she let it go. "Confer a little quieter next time, please, Mister Valentine."

"Absolutely," he said, nodding and leaning back in his seat oh-so casually.

Wendy fought so hard not to grin.

She was giddy—too little sleep on top of a world altering realization, and all before she'd had breakfast.

Covering her face, she leaned forward on her elbows and took deliberate breaths to center herself.

They'd figure out what to do. She'd weigh her options, maybe do some research on Pittsburgh cryptid sightings, check local papers and the like… She'd make a solid plan to take to Greg.

It would be a lot, but it could be done.

She hoped.

By the time class was dismissed, she was jittery again.

"Hey, so you bolted yesterday before I could get you to read over my article," Victor said, following her out of the room. "Want to take a look?"

Barely even aware of what she was agreeing to, Wendy nodded. "Sure."

She checked her watch. If she hurried, she had enough time to duck into the library computer lab before her other classes. It would mean skipping breakfast, but she was sure she could dig a few quarters out of her bag to get something from a vending machine.

"Great, thanks," Victor said, pulling a folder out of his bag. "So why did you leave so fast yesterday?"

Wendy blinked. "Oh, um, I had a... thing."

"An outdoors thing?"

"Huh?"

Victor gestured to her hair. "The twig, remember?"

"Ha, right. Yeah, kind of." Taking his article from him, she glanced over her shoulder, looking for an exit route. "Look, Victor..."

Wendy faltered, turning to face him.

Victor loved cryptids. Was obsessed, actually, and that was putting it nicely. He spent almost all his free time reading up on them—visiting message boards and talking to other monster enthusiasts.

He already had all the information Wendy needed, memorized and filed away in that hyper detail-oriented brain of his.

Wendy spoke before thinking. A dangerous maneuver for someone like her but desperate times…

"Victor, are you free tonight?"

He blinked owlishly, golden brown eyes catching the florescent lights.

"Uh, free, like… to do something?"

Wendy nodded. "Yeah, you want to, I don't know, grab dinner?"

Victor looked like she'd just splashed him with cold water.

"If you want, that is," she added, unsure.

"Y-yeah, yeah, of course," he said, reviving himself. "That sounds great."

Checking her watch again, Wendy started down the hall. "Okay, so I'll see you at six?"

"Sure," he called after her. "Should I change my shirt beforehand or…?"

Wendy frowned. "Um, if that makes you comfortable?"

Victor looked down at himself, tugging at the hem of his 'My friends went to Utah and all I got was this lousy shirt' tee. "I should change."

Wendy laughed to herself as she turned the corner.

Was it her, or did boys become stranger over time?

* * * * * *

July 1st, 2007

"Mama, can we go to the library?"

Darlene stirred creamer into her coffee, barely glancing over. "Story Time with Miss Kelly isn't until Saturday, hun."

Wendy took a huge bite of her Capt'n Crunch. "It's not for Story Time."

"Don't talk with your mouth full," Darlene said, sitting across from her. "Then why do you want to go to the library?"

Waiting until she swallowed, Wendy said, "I wanted to look up something. Isn't that what libraries are for?"

"Alright sassy-pants," Darlene said, fighting a grin. "We can go to the library."

Wendy had never gotten dressed faster in her life.

Yanking her shoes on, barely tying the laces, she bolted for her mom's Nissan. She buckled herself in and waited impatiently as Darlene gathered her purse and keys, calling out to John that they'd be back later.

The Mason County Public Library dazzled in the sun—tall white columns and front made almost entirely of windows beckoned everyone inside.

Wendy ran out ahead of her mom, passed the bell statue to the front door.

"Oh, hey, Darlene!" A woman called, waving at them.

Wendy only knew her as Jimmy's mom. Recognizable because she always wore the same floral dresses with the buttons down the front and white sneakers.

As Darlene slowed to make small talk, Wendy couldn't be bothered to wait.

A blast of air conditioning was a sudden relief from the humid summer. The smell of carpet cleaner and books filled her nose as she wandered by the computer tables and video rental racks near the front. Several people sat on benches or in the wooden rocking chairs by the windows, reading older issues of **National Geographic** *or some other grown up magazine Wendy didn't know.*

The brightly painted sign for the children's section was to her right, but Wendy continued walking. What she needed wouldn't be in the summer reading selections.

Wandering through the fiction section, weaving in and out of tall shelves piled high with books, she read the signs taped to the ends of each unit. Historical, Fantasy, Romance, Science Fiction…

A librarian Wendy had seen a few times during Story Time was organizing a stack of worn out murder mysteries.

Pulling her glasses off the top of her head, she muttered about them catching in her hair, before noticing Wendy in the aisle with her.

"Why hello there," the woman said, smiling. "Our children's section is actually back that way." She pointed in the direction Wendy had just came.

"That's okay. I have enough chapter books."

"Oh? Is there something else you're looking for then?"

Wendy straightened to her full height, hoping it made her look determined.

"I'd like to see all your books on Mothman, please."

* * * * * * *

The knock at her suite room door brought Wendy's head around.

"Just a second," she called, minimizing her browser window.

Victor waved as she let him in, and Wendy took note of his outfit change. Gone was the off-brand vacation shirt, and in its place was a striped, mostly wrinkle free button down. And his hair was combed—something Wendy wasn't sure she'd seen in the two years of knowing Victor. He usually just ran his hands through it and hoped for the best.

"Hey," she said. "You look nice."

He glanced down at himself. "Well, I wasn't sure where you wanted to go, and my mom always says it's better to be over dressed than under dressed, so…"

Pulling on her favorite jean jacket, Wendy quickly gathered up her laptop and notebooks.

"You're… bringing your stuff?" Victor asked, watching her shove it all into her bag.

"Yeah, I actually need your help with something." She hesitated. "It's kind of a side project."

Victor tucked his hands into his pockets, shoulders slumping oddly. "Oh. So this is a homework thing."

If she didn't know better, she'd have said he looked disappointed.

"No, it's not for school," she said, shaking her head. "C'mon, I'll tell you over dinner."

"We're not going to the cafeteria, are we? 'Cause it's fish'n'chips night and you know how I get with the smell…"

Wendy smiled, stepping into the hallway. "Gino's. Half-price pepperoni."

"See? This is why I like you."

Their favorite pizzeria just off campus was pretty slow for a Wednesday, and in no time they were chowing down.

Wendy hadn't realized she was so hungry until she'd nearly inhaled three quarters of the garlic breadsticks the moment they were in front of her. She managed to show a little restraint, leaving two for Victor.

He simply chuckled and dunked one in marinara.

Wendy waited until half of the pizza was demolished before broaching the topic she'd never entertained with Victor before.

"So, I was curious," she started, sipping her Coke. "Are there other beings around here other than Mothman?"

Victor froze mid-bite like an animal about to get hit by a Mack truck. "You're asking me about cryptids?"

Hoping she looked casual, Wendy shrugged. "The picture you showed me yesterday got me interested."

Furrowing his brow, Victor finished chewing before saying, "You've been listening to me go on and on about cryptozoology for two years, and you never once showed interest."

"I'm allowed to change," she said. "Maybe I'm trying to expand my horizons."

"You said, and I quote, 'Cryptids are hoaxes created by desperate people looking for fame and money.'"

Wendy rolled her eyes. "Vic."

"Another time I believe you said, 'Anyone willing to believe in things like Big Foot or the Loch Ness Monster should have their head examined.'"

"I didn't mean—"

"And then, 'Victor, no one will take you seriously as a historian or a journalist if you spend all your time hunting monsters.'"

Wendy jammed her straw into a clump of ice at the bottom of her glass. "You're making me sound like Doctor Bledsoe."

"You *do* sound like Doctor Bledsoe. You two could be voice twins, actually. It's creepy."

"Victor…"

Wiping the grease from his hands, Victor leaned his elbows on the table. "You're seriously asking me about cryptids right now? Like, as a legitimate topic of conversation?"

Wendy nodded. "I've clearly been… dismissive over the years," she said. "And they're important to you, right? You care about these creatures?"

He stared intently at her a moment before smiling. "Yeah, I do. I really do."

"Okay, then talk to me about them."

She'd never seen someone more excited to be given the greenlight to speak.

Victor's eyes lit up as he dove into his passion, explaining his love for the unknown, his delight at the idea that there were unidentified beings roaming the earth just waiting to be discovered, and his certainty that in the technology era there would be concrete evidence of their existence within the next decade.

Victor tripped over his own words, chasing tangent after tangent, but always coming back to his original point, all with impressive gesticulation.

He only bumped the pizza pan once.

Wendy smiled as she listened, as entertained as she was informed.

As he carried on, she pulled her laptop out of her bag, opening it up on the table.

"Uh oh, I've bored you so much you have to check Facebook," he said, hands folding in front of him.

"No, not at all," she said, connecting to the Wi-Fi. "I wanted to ask you what sites you use to keep up with all this stuff."

"Cryptid trackers?"

"Is that spelled how it sounds?"

Victor chuckled. "Uh, that's not… Here," he said, reaching for her computer. "I'll show you."

Opening several tabs, he brought up site after site before turning the computer around again.

"I put these in order of credibility," he said. "And in order of least annoying narrator."

Wendy scanned the first page, filled mostly with paragraphs of text. She recognized some of the names mentioned and stopped.

"This is about Mothman?" She asked, glancing up.

"Yeah," Victor said. "You're from Point Pleasant, so I figured I'd start with the posts about your own hometown cryptid."

Wendy opened her mouth but cut herself off.

It might break Victor's heart to know she'd been lying to him, that she'd already memorized all the information about Mothman she could find. Starting with the Birdman sightings, the encounters at McClintic wildlife management area, the year of Mothman, the bridge collapse…

Greg wasn't involved in the tragedy, and even a lot of locals agreed there hadn't been a Mothman sighting near the bridge that day, but he couldn't be detangled from the town lore.

"Have you ever seen him?" Victor asked, peeling a pepperoni off the pie and eating it.

"What?"

"Mothman. Have you seen him?" He faltered. "I mean, I assume you haven't, seeing as you're the world's biggest skeptic, but—"

"No, never," she blurted out. "Just the statue in the middle of town."

"Man, I can't believe you grew up in one of the biggest paranormal hotspots and you don't believe." Victor shook his head. "What a waste."

Wendy's gaze dropped to the grainy photo of a black winged creature at the top of the blog post. It wasn't of Greg, but it was a good fake.

If only Victor knew…

Chapter Four

A week went by and Wendy felt like a spinning top.

Every time her thoughts drifted, she was back on one of the sites Victor suggested, hunting for new photos of the Pennsylvania Mothmen.

She wasn't sure that was their real name, but it was what she was dubbing them until someone else came up with a better title. All she knew was they weren't *her* Mothman.

Studying the three credible photos she could find, she was able to decipher the main differences. The ones from Pittsburgh were a little smaller and leaner than Greg. Their wingspans were shorter too. And if she wasn't mistaken, one was more brownish-black than dark grey and black like Greg.

Wendy wanted nothing more than to run into the woods and show Greg each new thing she found, but the two-hour drive made that a little difficult.

She took comfort in knowing he was content back home, probably lounging in one of his favorite trees or other hiding spots, listening to the portable CD player she'd given him one year for Christmas, and eating his weight in Twinkies.

With barbeque sauce.

Together.

The thought made Wendy queasy. Greg loved the combination though, so she always brought him more, on the condition he wouldn't eat too many in front of her.

Focusing on her assignments and editorial responsibilities grew harder and harder as the week progressed. Wendy was turning into a compulsive phone checker, always scrolling her Google Alerts and any blog she thought was getting decent information, waiting for news.

After the fourth night of falling asleep on top of her laptop, she toyed with the idea of calling it quits.

Maybe the Pittsburg sighting was a one-off.

She even started telling herself it was a hoax, despite the eerie similarities the other Mothmen had to Greg.

And then, in the middle of her reheated breakfast burrito on Tuesday, Victor texted her.

"What the…"

The photo took a moment to download, but his caption was all she needed.

Victor: Still saying you don't believe? Guess who was spotted this morning...

Wendy gasped, choking herself on a partially chewed black bean.

"Oh my God," she croaked, chugging water and staring at her phone.

The creature looked just like Greg.

Immense, inky black wings, dark grey skin, talons at the end of long fingers, and red, reflective eyes.

Only this one was caught gliding off the Fort Pitt Bridge.

Adrenaline flooded Wendy's system, ruining her appetite.

It wasn't a hoax. There were other Mothmen. Several, if the photos were to be believed. Maybe a whole group—a family.

Greg's family.

He wasn't alone.

And now she had to tell him.

* * * * * * *

November 5th, 2007

Wendy tried not to cough as her mom took her temperature.

"Still high," Darlene whispered, reading the screen. "John, we might have to make a run to urgent care."

"No, mama," Wendy pleaded, looking between her and her dad. "I don't want to go."

"Sweetheart, you're sick," John said, sitting on the edge of her bed. "A doctor will get you sorted and you'll be right as rain."

"No, please," she said, tears welling.

Wendy hated doctors.

Going to a doctor meant needles and bad tasting pills the size of her head.

Darlene sighed, replacing the cap on the thermometer. "I'll go get her more baby aspirin."

Rubbing a hand over Wendy's sweat-matted hair, John attempted to convince her again.

"It won't be so bad, I promise. I'll be there to hold your hand. And I bet they'll even give you a lollipop for being such a good patient. Wouldn't you like that?"

Wendy considered it, but still shook her head. "I don't like doctors, daddy."

"I know, sport," John said. "I don't like 'em either. But sometimes we got to do things we don't like. We got to be brave."

When her mom returned with ginger ale and two Tylenol, Wendy was tucked back into bed to rest while they waited out her fever. As her parents left, her dad clicked on Wendy's giraffe lamp so she'd have a nightlight, and closed the door.

Wendy had just started to drift off to sleep when she heard a soft tap.

Ignoring it, she rolled her head on her pillow, but the sound grew louder.

Tap, tap…

Frowning, Wendy sat up in bed, staring at her window. The curtains had been drawn but through the small gap she saw something moving.

Two red eyes peeped inside, blinking at her.

Tap, tap...

"Greg?" She whispered, voice hoarse.

Tugging the blankets off her, Wendy quietly climbed out of bed and opened the curtains to see Greg's shadowy form crouched beneath the sill.

She smiled, big and bright, before coughing into her fist.

Holding up one finger to tell him to wait, she shuffled over to her desk. Silently moving her desk chair to climb onto, she unlatched the windowpane and pushed.

Cool autumn air hit her as she slid the glass up. "Greg, what are you doing here?"

Soft chirps, barely louder than a cricket's, answered her. **"I was worried. I haven't seen you for days."**

"I caught the flu," Wendy told him, careful not to lift her voice above a whisper. "Mama kept me out of school. She says I have to go to the doctor 'cause of my fever."

A large, dark hand reached up, gently cupping the side of her forehead.

"You're too warm." *He clicked.* **"Your mother is right."**

"Don't tell her that," Wendy said, leaning her chin on her fist. "She doesn't need any encouragement."

Greg's wheezing laugh made Wendy giggle.

Footsteps sounded from the hallway, and they both halted, looking towards her door.

"Wendy, honey, I'm going to check your temperature once more and if you're not better, we're taking you to get looked at." Darlene's voice echoed from the hall bathroom.

Turning, Wendy shooed Greg back. "You have to go. They can't see you."

"I'll hide."

"We pass right there to get to the car—"

Her bedroom door opened, and her mom stopped short. "Wendy, what in the world are you doing with your window wide open?"

Eyes darting to the shadow only she could see hiding in the flower bed, Wendy faltered. "Uh, I... I got hot. I wanted some fresh air."

Darlene frowned, stepping closer. "I wonder if your fever is breaking."

Jumping off her chair, Wendy rushed over so her mom wouldn't get too close to the window. "Does that mean we don't have to go to the doctor?"

Smiling, Darlene patted her cheek. "We'll see. C'mon."

But before she could uncap the thermometer, the backdoor slammed and she dropped it.

"Dar?!"

"John?" *She hurried back into the hall.* "What is it?"

"Did you see that?"

"See what?"

"That... That thing that just flew over the house!"

Darlene sighed, bending to pick up the thermometer. "No, of course I didn't. I was in here."

"Darlene, I saw him," *John continued.* "That was him, I know it was. It had to be."

"Saw who, daddy?" *Wendy asked around the plastic shoved under her tongue.*

"Mothman," *he breathed heavily.*

"Oh, John, don't start," *Darlene said, rolling her eyes.* "It was probably an owl, or a big bat."

"This was no owl, I am tellin' you..."

Wendy observed her parents volley back and forth about the winged creature that did or did not exist.

She stayed quiet on the matter.

"Why can't you just believe me?" *John asked, tone shifting.* "You hardly ever take my side—"

"I believe you saw something, John, but don't ask me to believe in Mothman," *Darlene said.* "It's nothing but a town myth."

"It ain't about that. You always got to cut me down when I'm tellin' you somethin'. Always—"

"That's not fair, John."

Wendy took the thermometer out of her mouth and hopped off the edge of her bed.

"Mama? Daddy? I want to go to the doctor."

Her parents froze, staring at her.

"You... do?" Darlene asked.

"Mhm hm," Wendy said, handing her the thermometer. "If they have to give me a shot, can we get ice cream?"

John grinned. "Someone's awfully brave all of a sudden."

Shrugging, Wendy looked back and forth between them. "Sometimes you got to be, right?"

Wendy did in fact have the flu, but she didn't need a shot.

They all got ice cream anyway.

* * * * * * *

Wendy tapped the end of her pencil on her textbook as she read, nervous energy too much for her body to hold inside.

"How's my new convert doing?"

"Huh?" She jerked her head up and was immediately met by Victor's cheesy grin. "Oh, ha ha, very funny."

Sitting across the table from her, he asked, "What're you working on?"

What *was* she working on? She'd barely retained anything she'd read in the last half hour. Her GPA was going to tank if she wasn't careful.

"Uh, just something for biology," she said, closing her book. "I think I need a break."

Victor tossed several notebooks onto the table. "Well, I am the king of procrastination. Want to play Twenty Questions? Oh, I know, let's play MASH. Maybe this time I'll end up with something other than a shack."

Wendy smiled faintly. "Victor…"

"Not your jam? We could make cootie catchers instead."

Before she could respond, his phone dinged, and Victor checked his notifications with earnest.

"This is probably a dumb question," he started, still reading. "But do you watch the show Paranormal Explorers?"

Yanking her hairband off her wrist, Wendy leaned back to pull her thick curls into a ponytail. "No, why?"

"'Cause they just announced they're doing a special about Mothman."

Wendy froze, hair half tied. "What?"

"Yeah, they're going to Point Pleasant and then up to Pittsburg to investigate the new sightings. They're supposed to be filming in, like, two weeks."

Victor flipped his phone around to show her the article headline.

As soon as she read it, her stomach dropped. She felt exactly like that day freshman year of high school when she forgot to finish a major project and only realized it when she sat down in class.

"You okay?" Victor asked. "You look kind of pale."

"Um, yeah, I'm…" She swallowed. "I'm fine."

Victor started to lean forward when something behind her caught his attention and he slumped back down in his chair.

"Oh no. Doctor Bledsoe is coming this way…"

Wendy turned to look. "So?"

"I may or may not have had a meeting with the Dean about prejudicial bias in the Anthro department…"

Wendy gaped at him. "You went over Doctor B's head about your stupid cryptozoology major?"

"I didn't have another choice," he whispered, contorting himself until he was nearly under the table.

"You're an idiot," she told him, reopening her textbook.

"Hide me—"

"Mister Valentine," Doctor Bledsoe called, heels clicking on the tile as she approached.

"Too late," Wendy said, looking up.

At five-foot three, Doctor Bledsoe was not particularly intimidating at first glance. But after spending two minutes with her, everyone came to the same conclusion—Doctor B was not a force to be reckoned with, even on a good day.

Victor had just swum into a hurricane.

"I understand you had a meeting with Dean Mitchell this morning," Doctor Bledsoe said, voice icy.

Straightening in his chair, Victor nodded. "I, um… Well, technically—"

"Technically?"

"I, you see, I… Yes, I did see Dean Mitchell, but—"

"Mister Valentine," Doctor Bledsoe started. "I understand you're passionate about this particular… topic. And while I am choosing to give you the benefit of the doubt in believing that it is that same passion that has blinded you in your efforts, I must say I do not appreciate being called up on accusations of *bias* simply because I will not greenlight a degree that serves neither you nor this university."

Victor shrank in his chair. "Yes, ma'am."

"If you have any other concerns, I'd much rather discuss them in my office, not in Dean Mitchell's. He has horrible taste in décor. Alright?"

Nodding, Victor couldn't form a reply.

"Excellent. I hope you enjoy the rest of your day," Doctor Bledsoe said, grin as sharp as a Ginsu knife.

Tilting her head, she softened her demeanor and greeted Wendy.

"I enjoyed your article about the recycling policies on campus last issue. Good work."

Wendy offered a smile. "Thank you."

"See you both in class," Doctor Bledsoe said before striding away.

Stock still, Victor stared into space, clearly dumbfounded.

"Breathe, Vic," Wendy told him, fanning him with a worksheet.

"That was a near death experience," he mumbled.

Wendy nodded. "Yeah. It was."

"She's terrifying."

"Yes, she is."

"I'm never doing that again."

"Good boy. You learned your lesson."

As Victor came back to himself, Wendy watched the color return to his cheeks, only to then burn bright up the column of his neck in a shade of pink that screamed 'mortified'. He hunched over the pile notebooks, opening one to attempt his homework.

Wendy blamed intense sympathy for what came out of her mouth next.

"Vic, have you ever been to Point Pleasant?"

He glanced up at her. "Uh, no, I haven't. I mean, I've wanted to, but I just haven't made it out there yet. Why?"

"Would you maybe want to come with me sometime?" Her heartrate spiked as her stomach swooped.

What was she doing?

What was she thinking?

What?

"This weekend, maybe?" She added, certain she was no longer in control of her faculties.

"You... You want me to go home with you?" Victor shook his head. "Sorry, that came out wrong. I meant you want me to go with you back home?"

Wendy nodded. "Sure. I could show you the town. You could get a taste of it all before that TV crew stirs stuff up."

If the wide grin plastered on Victor's face was any indication, his mood had certainly improved.

"Yeah, I'd love that."

"Great," Wendy said.

She'd officially lost it. There was no other explanation.

She just hoped Greg wouldn't judge her too harshly.

Chapter Five

Wendy needed the help.

At least, that's what she kept telling herself over and over. With Victor in the passenger seat, chattering away as they drove from Ohio State to Point Pleasant, she repeated the phrase to herself.

She needed the help.

She wouldn't be able to do this by herself.

Victor had proven he cared about the wellbeing of cryptids. He wasn't like the guys from that show he'd told her about—the same show Wendy ended up binge watching until two in the morning. He wasn't looking to get famous from a trumped-up scary story told in a dark room to a bunch of cameras.

She could trust him.

It was going to be a complicated effort to get Greg out of the McClintic Wildlife preserve, away from any film crews, and reconnected with his… Kin? Moth-people?

Wendy nearly chewed her lip raw by the time they crossed the town line.

She was queasy, sweaty, and for the last five miles she seriously considered flipping her car into a ditch to avoid all of this.

Get a grip on yourself, she thought. *You're doing this for Greg. He deserves to know his family.*

"I thought we were getting coffee first," Victor said, watching the quaint downtown area pass his window.

"Yeah, but first I thought you'd like to see the biggest hot spot," she said, gripping the steering wheel until her knuckles went white.

It was just like ripping off a Band-Aid. She was fussing over it but in the end, it might not be so bad.

Maybe. Hopefully.

Wendy really hoped she didn't puke.

Pulling onto the narrow road leading into the preserve, she took several deep breaths.

Victor's excitement was palpable.

"Oh wow," he said, arching his neck to stare out the window. "This is just as spooky as the pictures made it seem."

Spooky. Huh.

Wendy had never felt scared out there, amongst the fields and thick forest. It was her second home.

No, it was her first home. Her real home.

The preserve is where she truly grew up.

Parking, Wendy hesitated, hand on her keys.

"I need you to do me a favor."

"Okay," Victor said, still looking out the window.

Wendy turned off the ignition. "I need you to leave your phone here."

"What? Why?"

"Just…" She twisted in the driver's seat to face him. "Trust me?" She waited a moment. "Please?"

Victor squinted at her and then back out the windshield. "You're not going to murder me, are you?"

"No," she said, holding his gaze. "I promise no one will kill you."

"Is this some kind of townie initiation?" He asked, fishing his phone out of his pocket and dropping it into an empty cup holder.

She fought not to chuckle. "Not exactly," she said, pushing open her door and climbing out.

"Okay, but I have people who care about me and *will* notice if I'm missing," Victor called, struggling with his seatbelt. "And I have a lot of books due at the library, so please don't make my mom pay those fees."

"No one's killing you, Victor," she told him again, gathering the bag of bribes for Greg out of her trunk.

Twinkies, barbeque sauce, Jolly Ranchers, and the latest Taylor Swift CD, plus batteries.

A fool proof 'please don't be mad at me' kit.

Victor stared into her plastic bag. "I can't bring my phone but you're bringing junk food?"

"Don't snoop," she said, closing it and slamming the trunk door. "C'mon, it's not far."

"What's not?"

She didn't answer.

* * * * * * *

April 12th, 2009

"But Greg, it'll be perfect," Wendy called over her shoulder.

*The **shuuck, shuuck** of his wings through the grass sounded as he followed her, lumbering on all fours.*

"It's cold in there,"** he clicked at her. **"And damp."

"Well you don't have to stay in there all the time," she said, rolling her eyes. "But it's better than that abandoned building, and better than being out in the open."

"I like the open."

"Greg…" She groaned, turning to face him.

He always looked like a large, strange dog when he crouched.

"Wendy…"

"The TNT igloos are a perfect hiding spot," she said. "No one thinks you'll be there. I read all the books, and none of them mention the igloos—"

"'Cause I don't go there."

"Exactly!" She exclaimed, grinning at him. "So, no one will go looking for you there. Which means…" She gestured at him expectantly.

Greg lifted a coal black eyebrow at her. **"I'll stay safe,"** he grunted.

"That's right." Wendy spun back around, letting her hands graze over the tips of the tall grass.

"I've stayed safe for a long time, you know," he added, chirping as he hop-stepped along. **"No one's captured me."**

"People are only going to get nosier, Greg. Phones have cameras now. Good cameras. It's only a matter of time." Wendy slowed until she was next to him. "I'm worried about what might happen if someone finds out you're real."

Tilting his head up, Greg blinked in the sunlight. **"I know."**

Wendy's hand dropped to the bony curve of his wing, stroking like she would a cat. The fuzz that covered his torso was softest there.

"I love you, Greg."

Greg clicked happily. **"I love you too, Wendy."**

* * * * * * *

Damp leaves and twigs crunched under their feet as they walked.

"This is starting to look familiar," Victor said, stumbling through the brush. "I think I've seen pictures from out here. Is this—"

"Wait here," Wendy cut him off, stopping in a small clearing. "Don't move until I come back, okay?"

Victor furrowed his brow. "Seriously?"

"Yes, seriously."

"Wendy—"

Pointing at the ground, she said, "Stay right there. Got it?"

Victor gaped but relented. "Fine. Fine, I'll be right here… Waiting to get killed."

"No one is killing you," she sighed, turning to head in the direction of the igloo.

Greg trusted Wendy, trusted her judgement about people, and probably wouldn't think twice about her bringing someone else to the igloo to see him. But she couldn't stomach the idea of springing it on him without even asking.

And he was always more cheerful after a snack.

Reaching the overgrown entrance to the TNT bunker, she called out for him.

Heavy metal doors pushed open from the inside, hinges squeaking loudly.

Greg stuck his head out, one white earbud dangling below his chin.

"You're back so soon?"

Wendy grinned, hoping her nerves weren't evident. "You're not tired of me yet, are you?"

With two talons, Greg carefully removed the other earbud, wrapping the cord around his Panasonic portable CD player. With a quick tap of his nail, he turned it off, and stepped into the clearing.

"Of course not," he clicked. *"Is this about Pittsburg?"*

"Uh, sort of," she said, walking over with the bag of Greg-approved goodies. "Here, these are for you."

Dropping into a crouch, Greg set his CD player down in a patch of grass and took the gift eagerly.

Gleeful chirps erupted when he saw the Taylor Swift album.

"Is today a human holiday I don't remember?"

Wendy chuckled. "No, I just wanted to bring you something nice." Shifting her weight, she watched him tear into a wrapper, devouring the snack cake whole. "Actually… It's kind of a… bribe."

Pausing, with the bottle of barbeque sauce halfway to his mouth, Greg arched an eyebrow at her. He waited.

"Greg, I found out more about the Mothmen in Pittsburg," she started. "They look just like you. I studied the pictures pretty closely and there's at least two others. Maybe more. And I have a friend from school—"

"Victor?"

Wendy jerked her head back. "How did you—?"

He looked up at her knowingly. *"You only have one friend other than me."*

She gave an indignant snort. "That's not... Okay fine. So I'm not a social butterfly."

Greg's wet, wheezing laugh was made even more so by the mouthful of cake and sauce.

"Listen you," she said, crossing her arms. "This is kind of a big deal, so I need you to pay attention."

An affirmative chirp gave her the go-ahead.

"Victor helped me find out a lot, and I think... I *know* he'll do whatever he can for us. For you."

"Me?"

Wendy nodded. "Greg, there's a film crew coming in two weeks. They're going to search for you after looking into this new Mothman sighting. Things are going to get hectic and messy—"

"So?" He grunted, crumbs falling from his thin grey lips. *"Things were worse before. And now there are tours looking for me."* He shrugged, wings lifting up his back. *"Doesn't scare me any. I'm fine."*

"I know, but Greg... These other Mothmen, they're not hoaxes. They're like you, and..." She bit her lip. "What if they can tell you why you can't remember anything from before? What if they're family to you?"

Obviously disgruntled, Greg set the bag down, staring up at her in silence.

A knot the size of a softball swelled in her throat, cutting off her words and air supply for a moment.

Struggling to inhale, she finally spoke.

"We're family," she said, gesturing between them. "We'll always be family. But don't you want to know if you have family like *you* out there?"

His muddy red stare shifted to the grass a few feet by her shoes.

Wendy pressed on. "Greg, aren't you lonely?"

"Not with you."

"What about when I'm gone? I won't live in Point Pleasant forever."

He was quiet again, large hands gripping the plastic handles tightly.

Wendy swallowed down her tears. "I don't want you to go, Greg. It hurts just to think about it. But you deserve more than hiding in dark bunkers alone. I love you. This town loves you. But is that going to be enough for the next sixty years?"

Greg shifted on his haunches, gaze distant.

She thought he was going to argue with her when he suddenly blinked and looked up.

"Why did you mention Victor?"

Tucking her hands into her pockets, Wendy inhaled deeply.

Good thing he'd eaten.

* * * * * * *

Victor turned at the sound of her approach.

"Okay, so if this was some kind of test, I think I passed 'cause I really had to pee but I stayed right here like you told me to," he said, pointing to the ground.

"Sorry about making you wait. C'mon." She waved him over, holding a few thin branches out of the way.

Walking towards her, Victor glanced at her hands. "Hey, where's your bag?"

"Oh, you'll see," she muttered, leading the way.

The walk to the bunker was short, so she tried to prepare him as best as she could.

"Victor, there's something I haven't been totally honest with you about…"

He halted. "I knew it. You *are* going to kill me."

Wendy tossed her hands up. "Why do you think I'm a murderer?"

"Why did you bring me into the middle of the woods and make me leave my phone in the car?"

"I didn't bring you here to kill you, Victor. I brought you here to explain."

Some of the tension ebbed from his shoulders. "Explain what?"

Here it goes...

"The truth is... I wasn't as big of a skeptic about the supernatural as I let you believe," she said. "And after all the research we did, I realized... I'm going to need your help with something. Something big."

She tucked a stray curl behind her ear, glancing over at him. "But first, there's someone you need to meet."

Victor's forehead wrinkled in confusion. "Um..."

Before he could finish, they stepped into the larger clearing, facing the TNT igloo.

The bunker doors were wide open, creating a gaping, pitch black mouth in the middle of all the surrounding mossy green.

"Greg?" Wendy called, peering into the darkness.

Victor frowned at her. "Who?"

Echoing footsteps were his answer.

Backing away on instinct, Victor started to reach for her to pull her away from the perceived danger.

Wendy stayed put.

The footsteps grew louder, and before either of them could speak, Greg exited the bunker. Standing at his full height, he shook his wings out and stared down at them both.

"Victor," Wendy started, turning to look at him. "I'd like you to meet Greg." She waved a hand out as she introduced them. "You know him better as Mothman."

Tipping his head back slowly, gradually taking in Greg's enormous form, Victor barely breathed. All the color leeched from his face as he stared into Greg's dark red eyes.

Wendy continued. "Greg, this is my friend Victor from school."

It started as a barely audible whisper, hardly words at all. "You... You're..." Victor tried to swallow. "You're..." He gestured weakly. "That's..."

Greg ducked his head in greeting, clicking a *hello*.

"You..." Victor didn't finish.

Swaying, his eyes rolled back in his head. Knees buckling under him, Victor crumpled to the ground in a heap, managing not to hit his head on impact.

Wendy and Greg both jerked.

"Oh geez," she muttered, squatting down next to Victor.

Rolling him onto his back, Wendy grimaced.

"I guess I should have expected that, huh?"

Chapter Six

September 13th, 2009

Wendy dropped her backpack by the kitchen table, immediately looking to the clock on the stove.

Five minutes early. She was getting good at this.

"Wendy Kathleen Hyre!"

She froze, one foot barely an inch off the floor. Middle name, she was in trouble.

Her mother rounded the corner, fury personified as she entered the kitchen.

"You want to tell me where you were?"

Wendy lowered her foot. "I was at Rebecca's, mama."

"Don't lie to me, young lady," Darlene snapped, pointing at her with the end of her cellphone still gripped in her hand. "I called Mrs. Judson to ask you to come home early, and she said she hadn't seen you in weeks. And you've been telling me you've been over at Rebecca's every day after school."

Darlene folded her arms, glaring down at her daughter. It was the scariest Wendy had ever seen her mother look.

"So? Out with it. Where were you?"

"I..." Wendy began to shake. "I was with Rebec—"

"Damn it, Wendy, do not lie to me again!"

"Mama, I—"

From the living room, she heard her father get off the couch. "Whoa, hey now, maybe we bring down the volume a little, huh?"

Darlene stepped forward. "You tell me where you were, right this second, or you're never leaving this house again."

John sighed. "Darlene..."

"I mean it, Wendy," she carried on, ignoring him. "Where have you been going all those times you told me you were at Rebecca's?"

Panic bubbled in Wendy's chest.

She couldn't tell her the truth. Her mother would never believe her.

'Mama, my best friend is Mothman, and we see each other almost every day' was a statement liable to get Wendy, not only grounded, but institutionalized.

"There's a fort." The words catapulted from her mouth. "Out in the woods behind the ball field."

Her mother squinted at her. "A fort?"

Wendy nodded. "A lot of the older kids go there."

"Older kids," Darlene repeated.

John sighed. "Didn't she just say that, Dar?"

"I'm trying to get this story straight," Darlene said. Turning to Wendy again, she added, "You've been hanging out with older kids at some ramshackle fort in the woods?"

"It's... It's not like it sounds," Wendy said. "We just sit around and talk. Play games."

"What kind of games?" John asked, voice suddenly stern.

Wendy recalled her afternoon with Greg.

"Hopscotch."

It was her father's turn to glare at her. "You expect me to believe you were hanging out with older kids playing hopscotch?"

She swallowed roughly. "We climb trees too. And play catch."

Tossing her cellphone onto the counter, Darlene shook her head. "Fine, if that's the story you're sticking with, you were in the woods playing with older kids. Go to your room, you're grounded until further notice."

"But mama--!"

Darlene whirled on her. "You lied to me, young lady! You lied for weeks! I am so angry at you, I don't want to see you for the rest of the night."

Hot tears stung Wendy's eyes as she stooped to pick up her bookbag.

"Fine," she muttered, storming past her parents down the hallway to her room.

"And don't you slam that—"

*The door closed with a thunderous **bang** and Wendy chucked her bag across the room.*

As she cried into her pillow, she decided three things.

She'd never tell her parents the truth about Greg.

She'd have to learn to be sneakier.

And she needed better friends who weren't tattletales.

* * * * * * *

Wendy patted Victor's cheek firmly. "Vic? Vic, wake up."

Features pinching, he rolled his head from side to side.

"Ugghh… Man, I had the weirdest dream." Rubbing his forehead, he said, "I dreamt you took me into the woods to meet…"

Blinking his eyes open, Victor shouted in surprise.

In hindsight, Wendy probably should have had Greg wait in the igloo.

"Mothman!" Victor yelled, scrambling to stand up. "Mothman!"

Grabbing him by the shoulders, she tried to hold him still. "Victor, wait," she urged. "Calm down, it's okay. That's Greg, remember?"

On cue, Greg waved, and Victor paled like he was going to pass out again.

"That's... I... And you're..." He covered his face with his hands. "This isn't happening."

"I know this is a shock..."

"I can't believe this," Victor muttered. "That's Mothman. I'm meeting Mothman." Looking around at the patch of grass he landed in, he added, "I *fainted* in front of Mothman. This is the most embarrassing day of my life."

Wendy smiled reassuringly. "I'm sure that's not true."

"Junior prom is a close second. But this is definitely taking the cake."

Inhaling steadily, Victor forced his gaze up.

As he took in the sight of Greg in the sunlight, he trembled and a bead of sweat rolled down his temple. Wendy had to give him credit for keeping himself upright that time though.

"You're..." Victor swallowed audibly. "A legend."

Straightening with pride, Greg chirped.

Victor's eyes widened. "What... What was that?"

Urging him to his feet, Wendy explained, "He said 'thank you'."

"Wow. You really do sound like that, huh? Kind of like a mouse."

Greg furrowed his brows and snorted. A rapid set of clicks followed, and Victor immediately looked to Wendy for explanation.

"He doesn't think so," she said, holding onto Victor's elbow in case he got woozy again. As Greg finished, Wendy translated. "He says mice squeak and he certainly doesn't."

Worried, Victor looked up at Greg. "No, no, of course not. I didn't mean to offend—"

"Don't worry, he's not mad," Wendy chuckled.

Staring at her in awe, Victor inhaled. "You can understand him. How… How long have you known him?"

Glancing over at Greg, she smiled. "About eleven years."

The air between them changed, and Victor pulled free of her grasp on his arm. His once earnest and fascinated expression shifted into something brittle and closed off.

It made Wendy's stomach double over with knots.

"Eleven years…" Victor repeated, looking past her.

Panic—like the same kind she felt when she accidentally burned a frozen pizza and had to rush to open the doors and windows before the smoke detector went off—flooded her system.

"Uh, Greg, I'm going to talk to Victor for a minute, okay?" Wendy said, nodding to him.

Chirping in agreement, Greg turned, ducking back into his bunker.

Wendy wasn't sure she'd ever seen Victor angry.

Maybe once, in class, when he got into a heated debate with another guy who looked like an extra from a student film, complete with a beanie and paint splattered jeans. She couldn't remember what the argument boiled over into, but she remembered the look in Victor's eyes as he fumed.

It was the same look he was giving her now.

As he paced away from her, Wendy fiddled with her hands, biting her lip anxiously.

"You're friends with Mothman," he said, finally. "All this time…"

"Victor—"

"Do you have any idea what I'm feeling right now?" He dragged his fingers through his hair.

She took a step forward. "I know you're upset…"

"Yeah, I am." He turned on his heel, glaring at her. "All my life I've wanted this to happen, and now it has, and I'm too busy being mad at you to fully enjoy it. You've heard how everyone at school talks to me—Doctor Bledsoe thinks I'm an overzealous weirdo, people on the paper all think I'm some UFO conspiracy nutjob, and I can't walk into a single class without someone looking at me like I'm about to pull out a tinfoil hat to wear." Victor jabbed his finger in the air, punctuating each statement.

Wendy's heart sank to the pit of her churning stomach.

"And you…" He exhaled roughly. "You shot me down at every turn. Granted, you never made me feel *quite* as stupid as everyone else did, but you certainly didn't help. You made me believe you were a total skeptic, and now, come to find out you're friends with Mothman!" He pointed at the bunker as he yelled, and Wendy knew Greg was listening to every word.

"Victor, I never meant to hurt you," she said, moving closer. "But you have to understand… I only did it to protect Greg."

Victor made an indignant noise at the back of his throat, and for a moment her sympathy waned.

"What did you expect?" She snapped. "That I'd sit next to you in lab and introduce myself, 'Hi, I'm Wendy, I'm from Point Pleasant and I'm friends with Mothman'?"

"I thought you trusted me," Victor said.

"I *do* trust you," Wendy countered. "Why do you think I asked for your help? Why do you think I brought you here?" Trying to regain her composure, Wendy took a deep breath and held it. "Victor, I've never told anyone about Greg. Not even my own parents. Forget about the fact that no one would believe me, but think about what would happen if I drew more attention to him. I mean, Jesus, this town already gets swarmed every year for the festival, can you imagine what would've happened if I announced I spent my days after school playing hopscotch with Mothman? It'd be nineteen sixty-six all over again. Hunters with guns swarming the preserve, looking for a monster."

Victor crossed his arms, but he was attentive, listening to her argument.

"I've known Greg since I was nine years old," she said, tone softening. "He's my best friend, and I promised him I would do everything I could to keep him safe." She locked eyes with Victor. "Including lying to people I care about."

He stared at her a moment, anger ebbing out of his stance. "You're right. I shouldn't have gotten so defensive."

"I never meant to make you feel stupid," she said, brush crunching under her feet as she shifted her weight. "It's just easier if people think I'm a hard skeptic who doesn't believe in anything."

Tucking his hands into his pockets, Victor thought for beat. "Wait, you said you needed my help with something. Why would you need *my* help?"

"I figured someone who cared as much as you do about cryptids would be the best person to trust with transporting one," she said.

"Transporting?"

"The Mothman sightings in Pittsburg? They weren't Greg. Which means…"

Victor's eyes widened. "There are more Mothmen."

Wendy was starting to feel like she'd averted a disaster.

"Okay, I'll help," Victor said, walking towards her. "On one condition."

Alright, maybe not so much…

"I don't have a lot of money, Vic," she said. "So, you'll have to make your price modest at best."

"What? No, I don't want money," he said, shaking his head. "I want to study him."

"Excuse me?"

"Not in a gross, creepy way," he added. "Just, like, take notes on him. Get the facts about what Mothman—sorry, Greg—is really like."

Wendy scowled. "I'm not going to let you publish a story about him."

"It's for me," Victor told her. "Look, if these Mothmen are out there, getting themselves noticed, it's only a matter of time before someone accepts the reality that they're living creatures and not just myths. And when that day comes, I want proof that I knew. That I was there and have legitimate sources of information."

"Victor…"

"I just found out *my* best friend has been lying to me for two years," he cut in, holding her stare. "And now you're asking me for a favor. So, not to be an asshole, but you kind of owe me."

After a moment of serious deliberation, Wendy said, "You have to ask Greg for his permission first. And I know all your favorite online cryptid hangouts now, so if I see one thing written about Greg on there, I will hunt you down and upload a virus onto your computer that puts you back to pre-Y2K days, got it?"

"Deal."

Grinning, Victor started to walk by her.

"Vic?"

"Yeah?"

She worried her bottom lip between her teeth. "Still mad at me?"

The slope of his shoulders softened. "I won't be soon."

Wendy decided it was the best outcome she could have asked for just then.

"Want to reintroduce yourself to Greg now?"

He chuckled. "No second chances at first impressions, though, right?" Smoothing his hands down the front of his shirt, he gave himself a once over. "How do I look?"

"Like you've got a tinfoil hat in your back pocket."

"Oh, you're hilarious."

* * * * * * *

June 27th, 2011

"How long will you be gone?" *Greg clicked, swinging his legs from the branch he sat on.*

Wendy glanced up from her spot several limbs below. "A week."

"That's not so bad."

She sighed. "It feels like it'll be longer."

Greg swooped over, hooking his knees over the branch to hang upside down by Wendy's face. **"But it's a fun camp, right?"**

"It's a writing camp my teacher suggested I go to," she said. "I don't think there will be a lot of tree climbing but the brochure seemed nice."

Greg chirped in agreement. **"You'll probably meet lots of other kids who like writing just as much as you do."**

"It's just… I didn't ask to go," she said. "My teacher told my mom and handed her all these forms to fill out and then it was just decided. What if I wanted to stay home that week? What if I had plans?"

Wheezing out a laugh, Greg swayed on the branch.

"Hey, you don't know," Wendy said, pushing on his forehead. "I could be secretly popular, and you have no idea."

"Are you?"

Wendy pursed her lips. "Well… no. But still."

Flipping off the tree limb, Greg spread his wings and glided in a lazy circle around the trunk.

"I think it's a great idea," *he clicked as he passed her.* **"You'll spend a week learning new things and come back with amazing stories to read me."**

"They might not be that great," she said, watching him. "Maybe I'll write a bunch of bad poems. Then you'll really suffer."

Greg chuckled—a deep rumbling in his chest—and found a new branch to land on.

"I'll still love them," *he chirped. After a moment, he added,* **"I'll miss you though."**

Wendy swallowed. "I'll miss you too."

Chapter Seven

She heard him before she saw him.

Rapid, squeaking footfalls running down the corridor of the humanities building.

"Wendy!" Victor shouted as he barreled around the corner. "Wendy! Wen—Oh, there you are!"

She nearly dropped her books. "Jesus, Victor," she called, rushing over to him. "What's wrong?"

Panting, he let his backpack slip from his shoulder as he bent at the waist, catching his breath. "I think I have a plan."

"You ran all the way here, yelling my name like a lunatic, to tell me that?"

Victor nodded jerkily. "I had, like, three Red Bulls this morning, so…"

"You're officially never allowed to make fun of my caffeine intake ever again," she said, pulling him up by the shoulders. "Okay, from the top, a plan?"

"A plan to get Greg to Pittsburg while keeping your absences to a minimum."

Wendy frowned. "Why are you worried about my absences?"

"I'm not, but I know you are 'cause you're on scholarship and there's really strict attendance policies and GPA stuff you have to keep up with."

She halted, staring at his flushed cheeks and bloodshot eyes.

Had Victor slept at all since they'd gotten back from Point Pleasant?

"You remembered all that?" She asked.

An unfamiliar sensation rooted behind her sternum and Wendy stubbornly ignored it.

Victor shrugged it off. "Of course, I did," he said. "But look, I found a loophole."

Squatting down to dig through his backpack, he continued talking.

"You're in Professor Brown's propaganda and political theory class, right? Well, I'm in his Post-WWII America class." He retrieved a sheet of paper and stood up, swaying a little. "He handed this out this morning. It's a flier for a three-day symposium about civic duty, journalism, blah-blah-blah—The point is, he's giving anyone who attends an excused absence plus extra credit once you do a report on the event."

Wendy took the flier from him, scanning it quickly. "Oh my God."

Her enthusiasm was short lived, however.

"Vic, how are we supposed to pull off Project Greg at the same time we're at a symposium?"

He grinned. "'Cause we're not going to the symposium. My sister took his class five years ago and went to the same event. We're going to use her notes."

"What if her notes are outdated?"

Victor sighed, shoulders rolling back. "Then we'll find a YouTube video of the presentations or something. Wendy, you're missing the point, this is our way out." He tapped the paper vigorously.

Reading the details again, she glanced up at him. "It's next week."

"Missing the Paranormal Explorers film crew by a narrow margin, but still," he said. "This is our best option. Well, *your* best option. I was just going to say I had the stomach flu or a dead aunt or something."

"Victor."

"What? They're all dead already, so it technically isn't a lie."

"We'll discuss your greying morality later," she said, folding the flier up and tucking it into her pocket. "So, I guess, next week…"

"We reunite Greg with his long-lost Moth-kin."

Wendy nodded once, quietly absorbing her new reality.

It was happening. Greg would be leaving. Maybe temporarily, maybe permanently, but either way...

"Hey, you okay?" Victor asked, gently touching her elbow.

Wendy blinked. "Yeah, yeah, I'm fine."

It was a lie. A pretty bad one, if she was going to critique her fibbing skills.

Victor's nervous energy dissipated for a moment as he stared at her. "I know you're sad about losing Greg. It's okay to want the best for him and still be upset that it's happening."

"Until I moved for college, the longest I'd been away from him was a week. Maybe a couple of days if I couldn't sneak away to visit. I still forget I can't just hop on my bike and ride down the street to see him." Wendy inhaled deeply. "And now..."

Victor ducked his head, catching her gaze. "It isn't goodbye. It's just—"

"Later," she finished.

"Yeah," he nodded. After a moment, he glanced around. "Hey, are you busy right now?"

"No, my Lit class got canceled."

"Great, come with me," Victor said, tugging at her jean jacket sleeve.

They hurried across the quad, with Wendy only a few steps behind him. He wouldn't tell her where they were headed or what they were doing, but once she saw the library doors, she figured their options had narrowed.

"Over here," he said, guiding her to the row of computers. "Take a seat."

Eyeing him, she set her bag down. "Vic, what are we doing?"

"You'll see," he told her, rolling over another chair.

After pulling out a set of earbuds from his pocket and handing them to her, he opened the web browser.

"Stick those in and close your eyes."

Wendy looked from the headphones back to him. "Is this payback for this weekend? 'Cause you should know I hate jump-scares and I'm prone to punching when terrified."

Victor laughed. "Good to know for future reference, but no, that's not what this is. Now close 'em," he said, covering her eyes with his hand.

Wendy did as he told her, sitting rigidly in her wheelie chair.

Music started playing, and then a narrator began speaking in a soft British accent.

Victor nudged her and told her to open her eyes.

It was a video she'd seen clips of before on Twitter but hadn't taken the time to watch the full thing. The short, buzzworthy story of two men and the lion they raised from a cub.

The lion they eventually had to give away to protect, to give him a better life in a place he could call home.

The screen blurred and for a moment, Wendy hadn't realized she was tearing up. Then the moment when the lion recognized the two men after years of separation played out, and two streams rolled over her cheeks.

Taking one of her earbuds out, Victor leaned over. "See? Even lions remember their friends. So you know Greg is going to remember you too."

Sniffing, Wendy ran her fingers under her eyes to quickly rid herself of the evidence that she'd been crying.

"That was a dirty trick, Victor. It's not nice to make a girl cry when her mascara isn't waterproof," she joked, desperate to deflect.

"Nah, you look just as beautiful as always."

Wendy faltered.

Victor had called her beautiful before. It wasn't a forbidden word between them, weighed too heavily with implication.

But it was the softness in his voice, the tender way he let it blend into 'as always' that caught her off guard.

Before she could say anything, or even react fully, Victor cleared his throat, and pointed to the computer.

"Want to see a video of penguins falling down?"

She smiled. "Absolutely."

* * * * * * *

May 20th, 2010

Wendy settled with her back against a tree, bookbag next to her and notebook in her lap. Greg had promised to meet her there after school, and with how much she was struggling in social studies, she figured she'd take the time to study.

Digging out her CD player and new earbuds, she checked which album had been left inside.

She'd asked her parents if she could get an iPod for Christmas, but the expression on their faces had been more of an answer than their muttered 'we'll see'. So she settled for her tried and true while she saved her allowance.

Opening the case she carried her favorites in, she flipped through the plastic sleeves. It was filled mostly with Oasis albums borrowed from her dad, a couple Willie Nelson's records her mom had given her, and then the few she'd bought on her own.

The one she couldn't get enough of was near the back. Sliding it out, she popped it into the CD player, and hit play.

Adjusting the headphones in her ears, Wendy stared out across the small meadow, daydreams already taking hold of her.

The day never felt that bad when she could listen to music.

A soft tap on her shoulder jolted her, causing Wendy to dump her notebook onto the ground.

"Greg!" She turned to see him crouched behind her next to the tree.

"Sorry!" *He clicked.* **"I didn't see... What are those?"**

Tugging the earbuds out, she held them up to show him. "They're headphones, see? You listen to music through them."

Greg cocked his head, poking at one white wire to watch it sway. **"They're small."**

"That's kind of the point," she said with a chuckle. "Want to try? Here," she said, scooting over to give him room.

Folding his wings back, Greg settled in beside her, and waited for her to explain.

"You put them in like this," she said, showing him. "I think this will fit in your little ear hole, right there." Holding it up, she gestured to the side of his head.

Greg took the right earbud from her, and with a little fumbling, he managed to get it into the slit that served as his ear canal just under the sharp point of cartilage that shaped the rest of his upper lobe.

Watching his reaction, Wendy pressed play and adjusted the volume.

Black eyebrows shot up in surprise as he listened.

"It's Taylor Swift's new album," she told him over the melody.

Delight spread over his face as the song continued.

"Have you ever heard music before?"

"Not like this," he chirped.

"I love her. Want to listen to more?"

Greg nodded vigorously, glancing down at the CD player in her hands. It became an item of intrigue immediately.

Her social studies homework was forgotten, but Wendy didn't mind.

Not when the whole afternoon was spent listening to **Fearless** and laughing as Greg tried to sing along.

Chapter Eight

They fell into a rhythm.

Classes, schoolwork, continue to bribe Victor's sister for her symposium notes, eat something resembling nutritious, and plan for Operation Greg.

Surprisingly, it was a comforting routine.

Victor tapped the end of his pencil on the heel of his palm. "Okay, so we'll take my car."

Lying across her dorm bed, Wendy propped herself up on her elbows and squinted at him. "Why are we taking your car?"

"You drive a two-door Honda."

"And you drive a Subaru," she scoffed.

Victor stuck his nose up. "Though she be but little, she is fierce." He grinned and added, "Plus, I've seen Greg. There's no way we can fit you, me, and him into your Honda. Dude's a giant."

"Fine, but we should split up the driving," she said. "It isn't that far to Pittsburg, but we'll have a lot of ground to cover while we search."

Tipping back in the desk chair, balancing on two legs, Victor nodded. "Okay with me, as long as I get to pick the music."

"No way," she said, laughing. "You have terrible taste in music."

"Excuse me?" Victor kicked his leg out, nearly flying backwards. "My music taste is awesome."

"The last time you drove anywhere we had to listen to the *Avengers* movie soundtrack."

"It was a great movie."

"I'm not listening to EDM for four hours either," she said, watching his precarious chair positioning edge closer to an embarrassing tumble.

"Okay Miss high and mighty, let's see your Spotify," he said, hurling himself forward to snatch her computer.

Wendy tried, and failed, to stop him, but Victor was too fast. Immediately he was scrolling through her playlists—which to her was the equivalent of reading someone's diary.

"Wow, there's *a lot* of country music on here."

"I'm from West Virginia," she said, rolling her eyes. "What did you expect?"

"I definitely wasn't expecting this much Oasis." He glanced up at her, computer screen glow turning the whites of his eyes pale blue.

Wendy propped her chin on her fist. "My dad got me into them. He's seen them in concert twice."

"Clearly when the brothers were getting along."

She smiled. "They're kind of our thing."

After a moment, Victor returned her computer to her desk. "Alright, you can pick the music, as long as I get two vetoes an hour."

"One."

"Deal."

She shook her head. "Should've held out. I would have given you the two."

"Damn it," Victor groaned.

Wendy laughed, returning to her notes. She'd managed to write out a substantial list of possible Mothmen hiding places, where they might visit, and areas most similar to the McClintic Wildlife preserve. If they were anything like Greg, they'd probably gravitate towards the same kinds of locations.

"Wendy?"

She looked up from her paper. "Yeah, Vic?"

His gaze was suddenly earnest. Lips parted, like he was waiting for words to form, he hesitated.

"Uh, do you think…" But then he stopped, shaking his head. "Never mind," he murmured, turning his attention back to his notebook.

She wasn't sure of his original question, but she took a guess.

"Do I think we'll find them?" Wendy shrugged. "I'm not sure. Maybe. With Greg helping us, I think our chances are much higher."

Victor stared at her a moment, almost like he was confused, before he caught up.

"And what if we don't?" He asked.

Wendy pushed her curls off her forehead, fingers getting caught in the thick of them. "Then... I guess everything goes back to the way it was."

"Are you hoping we don't find them?"

She considered the question. "Sort of?" Her gaze dropped to the purple paisley comforter underneath her. "I want Greg to have family of his own. But I'm just selfish enough to say I won't be heartbroken if we can't find them."

"How *are* we supposed to find them?" Victor picked up the map he'd bought of Pennsylvania, unfolding it over her desk. "I mean, how did you find Greg?"

"By accident," she said plainly. "He saved me from falling off a concrete beam."

Victor stared in shock. "Oh. Sure. Seems typical." Shaking himself, he continued. "So, he was just hanging out, waiting to be stumbled upon by scrappy nine-year-old Wendy?"

She grinned. "Not exactly? I think I found his roost—or one of them. He told me he moved around a lot."

As she spoke, Victor began scribbling notes along the margins of his paper.

"Okay, and is he nocturnal?"

"No, but his circadian rhythms aren't like ours. He naps a lot, and only sleeps four hours at a time at night."

"Where are his favorite places to hang out?"

"You already know most of them," she said.

Victor tilted his head, looking at her. "No, I know what the cryptid trackers and blogs say. Now I have a direct source, so…" He tapped the corner of his notes with his pen, smiling.

Sitting up, Wendy swung her legs over the edge of her bed. "He likes thick forest—it's easier to hide in the branches. And water."

"Like the river?"

"Rivers, creeks, ponds… Water."

He nodded, taking dictation. "McClintic Wildlife reserve is his main stomping ground though, right?"

"It's home," she said.

She wasn't just speaking for Greg.

"Okay, so easy places to hide close to water…" Victor scanned the map. "The others are showing up near the river. But if they like to stay hidden mostly, why make themselves so obvious now?"

"Greg spent a full year getting noticed," she commented. "It's not that uncommon."

"Yeah, about that…" Victor set his notebook to the side. "Did he ever talk to you about that year? About all the sightings and the reports?"

Wendy swallowed. "Some, yeah. The thing is… Greg lost his memory. He told me he fell, and when he woke up, he couldn't remember anything. Didn't know where he was. That night he found four young people in a car and he tried to talk to them." She chuckled softly to herself. "But of course, Greg trying to talk to anyone at night is going to be terrifying."

"That was the Scarberry-Mallette incident." Victor leaned forward, pressing his forearms into the tops of his thighs. "They went to the cops, told them everything."

"There were sightings of a creature before that night, but when I asked Greg, he said he couldn't remember." Wendy tugged at the hem of her tee-shirt. "He might not know why, but he was living around Point Pleasant way before nineteen-sixty-six. And I think he had a job."

Victor's head jerked up. "Wait, what?"

"A lot of the places people saw Mothman were industrial—factories, mining areas, even military compounds. Most were places with machinery and chemicals…" She bit the inside of her bottom lip. "I think he was guarding them. Well, guarding the land, actually. And I think he was trying to warn people about impending accidents."

"Greg's psychic?" Victor nearly yelled.

"I don't know," she said hurriedly. "I don't think so. I think... I think he can just sense when something's going to happen."

"That's called being psychic, Wendy."

"He doesn't see it happening," she explained. "He feels it... Feels vibrations around him, can tell when something is instable."

A wide grin spread across Victor's face. "Are you telling me Greg can sense a disturbance in the Force?"

Wendy rolled her eyes. "You're such a nerd."

"Duh, you knew this." Grabbing his notebook again, Victor wrote a few lines. "So, all the people who think Greg is a harbinger of destruction..."

"They're wrong," she said firmly, the bad taste of decades of maligning against her best friend sticking in her throat. "I think Greg's a guardian. Like a gargoyle."

"He is much more reptilian than I was expecting," Victor said, nodding in agreement. "This is just..."

Her heartbeat tripped as she waited.

"So cool!" Victor beamed.

Relief evened her pulse out in an instant.

"All those years of reading about him, and now I get to spend four days with him on a road trip?" Victor flailed his arms happily. "This is my dream come true. Is this what meeting a celebrity feels like?"

"I'm not sure, but I'll let you know if I ever meet Tom Hanks."

Circling a few things on the map and underlining his notes, Victor murmured, "You're so lucky, Wendy. *The luckiest.*"

She wasn't sure if luck had much to do with it, but she'd be hard-pressed to argue the point.

* * * * * * *

October 20th, 2014

Wendy delighted in driving through the largest puddles she could find as she pulled into the McClintic reserve. With every splash of her tires, she grinned wider and wider.

"Greg!" She called out the window into the dark. "Greg, come look!"

A shadow separated from the treetops, swooping low. The graceful, bird-like flap of his wings was barely audible over the car engine.

Greg circled in a lazy oval before descending to the dirt road several yards in front of her headlights.

Wendy braked, pulling up close.

"I did it!" She exclaimed as she got out. "I passed my driving test!"

"Did they give you a car too?" *He chirped, cocking his head at the vehicle.*

"No, goofy, this is my dad's," she said, tossing the keys up into the air and catching them. "C'mon, let's go for a ride."

Greg looked from her to the car then back to Wendy. **"How am I supposed to…?"**

Wendy beamed. "This is how," she said, turning to push a button inside the car. As the roof began to recede, she smirked at Greg. "Well? What do you say?"

To the surprise of them both, Greg loved car rides. Took to riding shotgun like a happy dog, hanging his head out the window.

Hitting the gas, Wendy barreled them down dark backroads with Greg towering over the edge of the windshield. Arms up like he was on a roller coaster, he trilled and screeched as Wendy took sharp turns that would give her mother a heart attack.

"Hey, are you hungry?" She called up to him.

Clutching the frame of the car, Greg smiled down at her and nodded vigorously like a child.

"We're totally getting drive-thru," she said, making a turn and heading into town.

Her dad had left several CDs in the player, but she picked the Oasis one. It made for better driving music.

With "The Shock of the Lightning" blasting from the speakers, they B-lined for the glowing McDonald's arches.

"Greg, grab that blanket from back there," she told him as they pulled into the parking lot. "And hunch down."

Ordering for herself was simple enough.

Greg's tastes, however, were complicated at best.

And mildly disgusting at worst.

"Hi, can I get a number two with a coke, and..." She glanced over at the bundled-up guise Greg had managed for himself, and tried not to burst into a laughing fit. "Um, six quarter pounders, six filet-o-fish, two chicken nugget meals, and as much barbeque sauce as you've got."

"Sorry, how much barbeque sauce?" The cashier asked through a crackling speaker.

"All of it," Wendy said. "At least a bag full."

"Um... Okay. Please pull around."

The look on the window attendant's face was priceless.

Passing the first bag over, she squinted into Wendy's car. "All this for your... friend?"

Wrapped up like a Russian nesting doll, Greg kept his face hidden, as Wendy paid.

*"He's **very** hungry," she said, smiling.*

Four paper sacks later, and Greg's lap was full of greasy food and condiments.

"Have a great night," Wendy called, peeling away before anyone could see Greg's jet-black talons skewering several burgers at once and a carton of fries.

Stopping at a red light, she turned her head. "Hey, pass me my—"

Wendy gaped, watching Greg devour his food like he had a woodchipper for a mouth.

She wasn't even sure he was taking the wrappers off...

He still took the time to pour barbecue sauce on top of everything though.

"Never mind," she said, sipping her coke. "Don't drip on the seat or my dad will kill me."

Greg's grunt of an answer was a garbled, mid-bite collection of noises Wendy was surprised she could still understand.

Speeding away from town again, Wendy took them down as many two-lanes as she knew of, blowing past fields, tree lines, and occasional homes with the porch lights on.

Wet asphalt hissed under the tires as they raced downhill, towards one of the many desolate stretches of road. The further away from neighborhoods they were, the less likely it was for Greg to be seen.

Even in the dark, he was conspicuous—one of the down sides to having glowing red eyes.

As Wendy took a hard left, the road began to disappear in patches, replaced with gleaming pools.

It took her a moment to realize it had been flooded from the day's rain, mud and silt covering most of it with deep puddles that rocked the car when they drove through them.

Greg stopped, hand plunged deep in a bag, and his head jerked up.

Wendy glanced over, about to ask if he was okay. Then they hit a thick swath of mud and the wheel jerked.

It all happened too fast for her to comprehend much.

She could see bits and pieces in the narrow scope of her headlights.

The washed-out road.

The wide oak tree they were headed straight towards.

The mess that had become too slick for her tires to grip.

A powerful whoosh of air hit the side of her face as Greg's wings snapped out like a huge sail.

Bracing himself against the seat, his wings became a parachute, creating enough drag to slow the car. Wendy gripped the wheel and straightened it, keeping the car on the road with only a slight bump as the right tire went off the shoulder.

She let off the gas pedal immediately, rolling to a stop several yards away from the scene of their would-be accident.

With knuckles so white she could see them in the lights from the dash, she stared numbly at the darkened lane ahead of them.

"That... That was..."

Greg tucked his wings back behind him, settling into the seat once more.

"We almost..." Wendy twisted to look at him. "You saved us!"

Big, reflective eyes blinked at her once before he shrugged. **"I felt it coming,"** *he chirped.* **"No big deal."**

"Greg! Are you kidding! That was a mir—"

Before she could finish her manic rambling, a burger still in its wrapper appeared in front of her face.

"You going to eat this?"

She shook her head. Greg had earned it.

Chapter Nine

Wendy smelled the coffee before she even noticed the seat next to her was no longer empty.

"I made it a large," Victor whispered, careful not to disrupt the study group. "You looked like you could use it."

She glanced up, coming back to reality.

"Are you telling me I look tired?" She asked, taking the coffee from him. "Because that's not even remotely a compliment."

Victor's mouth fell open, clearly at a loss. "No, of course not, you just look… less rested than usual."

"That's not any better."

"Sorry, I just… could tell you were struggling a little."

Wendy rolled her eyes. "You can go now."

"Hey, I'm not sleeping either, so you're not alone."

Sipping the latte, she was surprised it was exactly how she liked it. Had she ever told Victor her coffee order?

Staring at him over the plastic lid, she said, "What do you have to be nervous about?"

"Uh, let's see, packing up a legendary cryptid, taking him four hours away to a city to find others like him, and also trying not to be spotted by people or cameras or both. Not to mention the hiking element."

Wendy smirked. "You're afraid of hiking?"

"Look at me," Victor said, waving a hand in front of his band tee shirt clad torso. "What about me screams 'outdoorsy' to you?"

"You'll be fine," she chuckled. "Just look for snakes and poison ivy and don't run from bears."

"*Bears?*"

An annoyed junior at the other end of the table shushed them and Wendy mouthed an apology.

"Bears?" Victor repeated in a whisper, eyes wide.

Wendy shook her head. "I was kidding. Mostly. Don't worry about it."

"Cool, great, loving the additions you're giving to my nightmares."

Eyeing the other students at the table, she said, "Are you actually going to study or did you just swing by to freak yourself out more?"

"The latter," he said. "I've got an article and an essay to finish before tomorrow, and we both know my frantic deadline typing scares the nervous freshmen."

Tomorrow. The word hit Wendy like a sack of rocks to the gut.

"Want to get food when you're done?" Victor asked, standing up.

She thought about saying no. She still needed to pack, and finish another assignment… But she couldn't ignore how the idea of being by herself all evening made her insides squirm.

Wendy nodded.

"Thanks for the coffee," she added, smiling up at him.

"Any time," he said, saluting her with two fingers.

A lot like Greg would do.

Wendy focused on the paper cup, where the curl of the Y at the end of her name disappeared around the edge.

Tomorrow, for better or worse, would be the end of a chapter.

And the start of a new one.

* * * * * * *

April 10th, 2012

Wendy hadn't noticed the sun go down.

Hadn't noticed her room plunged into grey dusk.

She only noticed the way her throat ached, and eyes burned.

It hadn't made any sense to her. Not really.

She knew things were strained, they'd always been like that, but…

Pulling her knees up to her chest, she pressed her forehead to them, cradling herself through the tears.

A familiar tap at her window brought her head up. Blinking, she squinted into the darkness.

"Greg?" She whispered.

Climbing off her bed, she quietly pushed open the window, leaning over the sill.

"What are you doing here?"

Big, red eyes stared up from the bushes. **"We were supposed to meet at the creek today,"** *he clicked.* **"I was worried."**

Wiping her cheeks, Wendy sighed. "I'm sorry, Greg. I forgot."

"What's wrong? You're crying."

Exhaustion had her trailing back to sit on the edge of her bed.

She stared at the floor a few feet away. "It's been a long day..."

Black clawed hands wrapped around her ivory windowsill as Greg pulled himself up and over. Landing as quietly as possible, he stayed crouched in front of her. He was much too big to stand upright in her bedroom.

"What happened?"

Wendy swallowed around the knot in her throat. "My parents are getting divorced."

Greg stared up at her, uncertainty drawing his eyebrows together.

"It means…" She sniffed. *"When two people are married, they're together. They say vows and… They choose each other. When people divorce, it means they're…"*

Tears fell from her lashes, rolling over her cheeks.

Greg inched closer. **"Divorce means… not choosing each other anymore?"**

She nodded. "Yeah. That's what it means."

"What about you?"

"Dad said we'll still see each other," she explained, wondering just how much a creature like Greg understood about child custody arrangements. *"Mom and I are staying here, in the house…"*

"I meant… Do you choose this too?"

Wendy shook her head. "It's not really something kids get to choose," she said. *"It's more like something that… happens to them."*

Sitting back on his heels, Greg held her gaze. **"That sounds… painful."**

"It is. It really is." More tears flowed as Wendy nodded.

Calloused fingers took her hands, squeezing them gently. **"I'm sorry, Wendy."**

"Thanks, Greg," she whispered through a sob.

For all Wendy knew, they sat like that for hours. It was probably more like minutes, but time didn't feel very concrete to her. Like trying to get her bearings while on a Tilt-a-Whirl.

Finally, she wiped her face with the sleeve of her shirt and looked at Greg.

"Will you... Will you stay?" She asked. "I know it's kind of risky, but I really don't want to be alone right now."

Greg nodded, thin dark lips curling into as soft of a smile as he could manage. **"Do you have your headphones?"**

Grinning, Wendy stood up and snagged them off her nightstand. "T-Swift? Or Netflix binge?"

"Both?"

"This is why we're friends," she said, climbing onto her bed while Greg made himself comfortable on the floor next to her.

Tossing him a blanket, she waited for him to be cozily wrapped up before hitting play on the next episode of **The Office.**

They made it through two and a half episodes before Wendy's eyelids drifted closed.

When she awoke, the first thing she noticed were the white cords of her earbuds dangling between her and Greg. The twinkle lights over her headboard gave enough light for her to see Greg's long legs stretched out along her floor, the throw blanket she'd given him barely reaching his knees.

The show had paused, with a pop-up window asking if they were still watching.

Night had fallen, the sky outside her window an even deeper inky vastness.

Wendy started to sit up, about to hit 'play', when her hand caught in something.

Something was holding her.

Craning her neck to see over the edge of her mattress where her arm dangled, she saw Greg had dozed off too, arm propped up on her bedframe so he could hold her hand.

Slowly, so as not to disturb him, Wendy adjusted the volume on her laptop and started the next episode. She kept her arm exactly where it was, hand fully grasped in Greg's.

When sleep took her again, she didn't fight it. She knew Greg would be there the whole night.

* * * * * * *

The knock at the door made Wendy's stomach clench. *Go time.*

As she opened it, she attempted an air of cheeriness as she greeted Victor.

"Morning," she said, smiling.

She was convinced it looked more like a grimace.

That's how it felt anyway.

"Morning." Handing her the second coffee he brought, Victor glanced around. "Hey, how come I never see your roommate?"

"'Cause she's always with her boyfriend," Wendy told him, turning to grab the last few things she hadn't packed. "She only stops by for clothes or to get a book she needs."

"Wow, you're living the dream. It's like having a single for the price of a double."

Wendy smirked, stuffing her conditioner into her already full toiletries bag. "Jealous 'cause your roommate is on the basketball team?"

"The five AM wake up calls are brutal," Victor groaned. "And our fridge is always full of Gatorade and protein shakes."

"You're right, you're clearly living in Hell."

He rolled his eyes at her. "Don't mock from an advantage point. It's just mean."

Wendy laughed, hoisting her bag onto her shoulder and grabbing her suitcase handle.

She gave the room a once over, certain she was probably forgetting something but unable to decide what it could be.

"Ready?" Victor asked, offering his hand to take her bag for her.

Trying not to be too obvious with her surprise, she let him carry her suitcase. "Yeah."

"The USS Greg is officially leaving the station," he called, stepping into the hallway.

"Port. Ships leave port, not stations."

Victor sighed. "And we're off to a great start."

Chapter Ten

Greg was already waiting for them outside the concrete bunker like a child ready to get picked up for camp. A plastic bag filled with the rest of his Twinkies and barbeque sauce, and his portable CD player was sitting at his feet where he crouched in the grass.

Waving as they entered the clearing, Wendy smiled. "You ready for a road trip?"

"I packed my essentials," Greg said, grabbing the handles of the grocery bag and holding it up. *"Will there be time to stop for lunch? I'm starving."*

"You're always starving."

"Exactly."

Swatting an insect off his arm, Victor scowled. "I should've brought bug-spray…"

"I have some," Wendy said. "You can't spray it around Greg though. It stings his nose."

Making a noise at the back of his throat, Victor pulled out his phone and started typing a note. "Hates… bug-spray…" He muttered.

Lifting an eyebrow, Greg glanced at Wendy. *"Is he going to do that the whole time?"*

"Unfortunately."

Victor looked up from his screen. "Are you talking about me?"

"No, of course not," Wendy lied, shaking her head.

Stare bouncing between her and Greg, Victor squinted. "Convincing."

"C'mon, we better head out."

Turning, she smirked as Greg shrugged his shoulders, wings bobbing behind him.

The walk back through the preserve was quiet, save for the occasional grunt from Victor when he tripped on a root or hidden stump. When they were getting close to the entrance, Wendy glanced over at the others.

"Okay Greg, we're going to have to move fast," she started. "It's a nice day, so I'm sure people will be coming and going and—"

She pulled up short at the tree line.

Shit.

The once empty parking area was filled with vans. Groups of people were milling about, making all sorts of noise.

"Vic…"

Pushing aside a branch, Victor peeked through the leaves. "Oh no."

"Is that who I think it is?" Wendy asked.

"Paranormal Explorers," Victor confirmed. "I recognize the logo."

"You said they'd be here *next* week."

He released the branch with a bounce, barely grazing his cheek. "It's not like I have access to their production schedule," he whispered. "I just read the blogs like everyone else."

"Well now they're here," she said, waving a hand out. "And we have to get Greg into your car without being seen."

"That's a lot of people to sneak around…" Greg chirped, ducking further down to stay hidden. *"What do we do?"*

Wendy didn't have an answer.

Looking up at Victor, she asked the same question. "What do we do?"

"Uh…" Victor turned, gaze darting from trees to parking lot to the sky. "Is there another way out of the preserve?"

"Not one that leads to the car."

"I meant for Greg," he added. Facing him, Victor asked, "If we can get the car and somehow get to another side of the preserve, could you meet us? Without being seen?"

Greg clicked, and Victor glanced at Wendy.

"He said yes," she translated. "Greg, are you sure?"

"I'll have to glide from tree to tree instead of fly, but I think so."

Victor frowned. "Was that another yes?"

"He can do it," Wendy said. "Greg, meet us on the north end of the preserve, by the turn off. Okay?"

Handing his bag of necessities to Wendy, Greg nodded before taking off at a gallop on all fours, leaping through the brush.

Victor gaped after him. "He can do *that* too?"

Tugging at the sleeve of his plaid shirt, Wendy ushered him through the trees into the parking area.

The car wasn't too far from the trail, but unfortunately that put it right next to one of the Paranormal Explorers' vans.

Attempting to look casual, Wendy and Victor strolled by the camera crew setting up their equipment. No one in the cluster noticed them, and she thought they'd manage to make it past without incident.

She was very wrong.

"Oh, hey, guys!" A voice called to them from further away. "Hey, can we talk to you for a second?"

Victor winced. "Busted."

Looking over her shoulder, Wendy faked a smile at the man jogging over.

"Just be cool," she said under her breath.

"Please, I'm always cool."

The closer the man got, the more familiar he was to her. Wendy recognized the dyed black hair, goatee, and omnipresent dark clothing that either came from Hot Topic or a motorcycle shop, she wasn't sure which.

He was one of the hosts of the show—Darren or Derek. Something like that.

"Hey, thanks for stopping," the man said, extending a hand. "I'm Devon."

Wendy nodded subtly to herself. *Devon, right.*

"I'm one of the hosts of Paranormal Explorers," he continued. "Would you two mind if we ask you a few questions for the show?"

Scrunching her nose, Wendy spoke. "Actually, we were just—"

"Absolutely!" Victor nearly cheered, beaming like he'd won the lottery.

He'd been a little off his timeline, but Victor was right. Wendy *was* going to murder him.

"Except we have that *thing* we have to get to," she said, staring at him intently.

"It'll only take a few minutes, I promise," Devon said, adjusting his sunglasses on top of his head.

The amount of sterling silver jewelry on the man's hands was astounding. How did he do anything with that many rings on?

"Yeah, let's do it," Victor agreed, already following Devon back towards one of the vans.

Wendy grabbed him by the arm, nearly yanking him off the ground. "What are you doing?" She whispered harshly.

"Living out a childhood dream," Victor said once he regained his balance. "And giving Greg time to get to the other side of the preserve before these guys head into the woods looking for him."

She wouldn't admit she was wrong, especially since she didn't believe she was in that moment, but Wendy conceded that Victor's idea wasn't terrible.

Reckless, and a bit ego driven, but not terrible.

Her realization must've been painted all over her face because Victor's grin was just shy of shit-eating.

"You're welcome," he said, leaning in.

Turning, he sauntered towards the camera crew.

Wendy exhaled loudly. She was still revoking his music vetoes later.

Hanging back, she kept her arms crossed and a perma-frown etched into her features. She didn't want anyone to get the bright idea she'd be game for an on-camera interview too.

The camera men set up while a woman gave Victor a quick pat down with powder and adjusted the collar of his plaid overshirt.

He looked absolutely giddy as they mic'd him and offered a few words of 'don't be nervous' and 'pretend the camera isn't there,' encouragement.

As a producer lined up the shot, Devon glanced at Wendy. "We're not getting you into hot water with your girlfriend, are we?" He asked Victor with a smile.

Victor's eyes went wide. "Oh, uh, she's not—"

"No, not at all," Wendy cut in. "I'm just camera shy."

The less they talked to her and about her, the sooner the host could interview Victor.

And that meant the sooner they could leave.

"Gotcha," Devon said, making a finger gun motion at her. "Okay, well don't worry. We'll make this quick."

Thank God, she thought.

Victor started to sweat as they rolled camera, and the questions came one after the other, jumping right into the meat of the Mothman mythology and the town's history.

To his credit he managed not to ramble too much.

"So, you believe in Mothman?" Devon asked, just in frame enough to make himself noticeable.

Big brown eyes found Wendy's.

"Yeah," Victor said, nodding. "I do."

"Are you afraid of him? Does the idea scare you?"

"Not at all," Victor said. "I think…" He looked over at Wendy once more. "I think if he's real, he's very misunderstood. Maybe more like… Like a gargoyle than a harbinger of destruction."

Wendy smiled softly, hearing her own words repeated. And on video, no less.

With a few more questions, the interview wrapped. The producer called 'cut' as Devon shook Victor's hand heartily. Before he could slip away though, Devon took two bags of show swag from a bored PA and handed them over. Inside the show logo totes were Paranormal Explorer tee shirts, stickers, a plastic to-go cup, and key chains.

"Everything I've always wanted," Wendy muttered.

Victor was too distracted with the shirt, holding it up to himself, to notice her sarcasm.

"Thanks Devon!" He called, waving good-bye, as Wendy dragged him around the side of the van to the car.

Climbing in, she tucked their bags under her seat while he pulled out of their parking spot. Careful not to kick up dirt or gravel, he sped as fast as he could manage out of the lot.

"That was so cool!" Victor beamed, turning onto the road. "Did I sound okay?"

"You did great," Wendy said, arching her neck to look out the open window, scanning the tree line. "Greg?!"

Victor stared at her. "Should you be yelling for him like that?"

"What, like yelling the name Greg is suspicious?"

"Well it certainly isn't inconspicuous."

"It's not like I'm shouting 'Mothman' at the top of my lungs," she said, still watching for a familiar dark form. "Greg!"

Just as she faced forward, something darted into the road in front of them.

"Victor!" She cried, bracing on the dashboard.

Slamming on the breaks, he waited for the collision that never came.

A moment later, two reddish-brown eyes blinked at them over the hood of Victor's car.

"Holy shit," Victor gasped. "Holy *shit*."

Throwing her door open, Wendy jumped out. "Greg?"

"Should I have waited for you to stop?"

"Yes," she exhaled roughly. "That probably would have been best."

"Sorry."

"C'mon," she urged, opening the back door for him to climb in. "Hurry before someone drives by."

As Greg maneuvered his limbs and wings into the back of the Subaru, Wendy got in and buckled up.

Still shaken, Victor ran his hands through his hair. "I can't believe I almost hit Mothman with my car."

A large black claw landed on Victor's shoulder, patting him reassuringly. *"You wouldn't have been the first."*

Looking from Greg's hand to Wendy, Victor waited for translation.

She sighed, sinking deeper into her seat.

"It's okay, Vic. Just drive."

Chapter Eleven

July 11th, 2011

"Mama, I'm too old for Vacation Bible School," Wendy groaned from the passenger seat, head thunking on the window.

Darlene adjusted her grip on the steering wheel. "Which is exactly why this year you're a helper."

"A **junior** helper. I'm not even a regular helper. Those girls get to lead the games and teach songs, and I'll be stuck passing out snacks and juice boxes and taking the really little ones to the potty."

"Sweetheart, I know it might not seem like it now, but you're going to look back on these days when you're my age and wish you'd had more of them 'cause they were the most carefree days of your life."

Wendy rolled her eyes. She didn't want carefree. She didn't want to help change pull-ups in the handicapped bathroom in the church fellowship hall.

She craved the smell of the woods around her. Wanted to be draped over a fallen log as she stared up at the sky, deciding which clouds looked like which celebrities. Or animals. Or both.

She wanted to spend her days exploring with Greg.

As they drove by the sign for the McClintic Wildlife preserve, Wendy sighed again.

Hi Greg. Bye Greg, *she thought, watching the grass blur by her window.*

Her mother had just started explaining how Wendy needed to spend her time productively during summers, and that going off into the woods to do whatever she wanted wasn't grooming her to be a helpful church member, when she saw something out of the corner of her eye.

A blackish grey figure, much larger than any deer or dog, running alongside their Nissan.

Wendy nearly gasped, but choked herself on it.

She recognized the creature, even if he wasn't flying.

Smiling out the window, facing totally away from her mother, Wendy stared as Greg ran on all fours, dodging and weaving through the trees and tall grass.

"Wendy, are you listening to me?" *Darlene asked, annoyed.*

"Huh?" *She twisted to glance over at her mom.* "Oh, yeah."

"Very convincing…"

Wendy's attention was firmly on the acrobatics Greg was doing outside, joyfully leaping and gliding before dropping back down into a gallop.

Letting his wings catch enough air to glide for a few seconds, he tilted his head and smiled—an act that would scare anyone but Wendy—and waved at her.

Covering her mouth, she stifled a laugh.

He'd felt her nearby. He'd come to say hi.

"Some days I feel like you and your daddy both think I talk for my health," Darlene said, sighing heartily. "I just love wasting my breath…"

"Sorry, mama," Wendy said, looking over at her.

Wiggling her fingers in response was the most she could, but Greg clearly saw. He waved again before slowing his gait, ducking out of sight.

She bet nobody else at Vacation Bible School had a best friend who could fly.

* * * * * * *

Parked on the side of the road about two miles away from the preserve, they regrouped.

"Here's your stuff, Greg," Wendy said, handing the plastic bag over.

Twisting in his seat, Victor glanced back. "How you doing back there?"

Bent awkwardly at the neck, with the side of his face pressed against the car ceiling, Greg stared at him. Lifting one eyebrow, he clicked in an annoyed tone.

"Uh, I'm guessing that's not an 'I'm peachy' sentiment."

Wendy shook her head. "Greg, scoot down and put your feet up here."

Victor made an aghast noise, watching Greg shuffle around. "Wait, what?"

"He's eight feet tall with wings," Wendy said. "What else is he supposed to do?"

With that, Greg unfurled his long legs, propping his giant clawed feet up on the dashboard. Smearing mud or some other viscous substance on the LED clock screen, his big toe accidentally changed the radio station and turned the heater on at the same time.

Victor's features pinched in disgust. "Ugh, what the hell… Dude, I'm not trying to shame you here, but your feet are gnarly."

Lounging back, Greg arranged his wings so that they spread out by his sides, and grinned at Victor's obvious distress.

"It's not like he wears shoes," Wendy said, picking Greg's foot up to change the station back and turn off the heater.

"He knows how to use a CD player but you never taught him about a nice Epsom salt foot soak?"

Greg chirped, and Wendy turned to look at him. "It's not nearly as fun as it sounds."

"Uh, she's lying," Victor countered. "It's delightful."

"Would you please just drive?" Wendy sighed, waving an arm out at the road ahead of them.

"Alright, alright…" Turning the ignition, Victor pulled onto the asphalt.

The closer into town they got, the more she felt Victor's stare on her at any possible moment. Concern knit his brows together as the minutes passed.

"What, Victor?" She finally asked.

"Nothing," he said, shaking his head. After a beat, he continued. "I just wanted to see how you were doing."

"Me? I'm fine. You should be asking Greg how he's doing."

Crinkling plastic could be heard from the backseat as Greg unwrapped several Twinkies and held them in one hand. Dousing them all in barbeque sauce, he purred like a hungry house cat. At the sound of his name, however, he stopped with the snack cakes an inch from his mouth.

"That is so gross," Victor laughed, facing the road again.

Wendy smiled. "He knows."

As the song on the radio changed, Victor glanced over at her once more. "Hey, I know we're on Operation

Greg's Moth-kin here, but did you want to swing by and see your parents? Since we're in town—"

"Nope," she interrupted, shaking her head.

"You sure? I mean we're only—"

"I said no," she snapped.

The atmosphere inside the Subaru pressurized.

Greg's eating slowed and he grew quiet, looking from Wendy to Victor and then back again.

"Okay..." Victor said after a moment. "Just thought I'd ask."

Minutes felt like an eternity as Wendy stared out the window, watching the grass blur.

Inhaling deeply, she leaned back in her seat.

"Sometimes it's easier not to see either of them," she started. "Ever since they got divorced, it feels like... If I go to lunch with my dad, my mom thinks I'm avoiding her. And if I spend the night with my mom, my dad feels lonely and left out. They act like I'm picking sides, even if they don't say it, and it's just... easier to avoid that all together."

Victor nodded in silence, absorbing what she said.

"I get that," he said finally. "Well, I mean, not exactly. My parents are still together to the point of being sickening at the dinner table. But I get wanting to avoid conflict. Sometimes neutral territory is easier to navigate."

It had been a while since she'd admitted her truth about her parents' split.

It was a complicated situation, wrought with tension and frustration and a lot of anger. And that was just on a good day.

Most people were too uncomfortable to discuss it with her for very long. Some acted as if she should cut her parents more slack or work harder to move on.

She hadn't expected the sudden relief she felt when Victor didn't balk at her words.

"I'm sorry," Victor murmured.

"For what?"

"That sounds really hard. Feeling torn like that."

Wendy smiled weakly. "Yeah, it is. But it's not all bad."

"Oh yeah?"

Desperate to lighten the mood, she said, "I get two Christmases, two birthdays, and loads of 'sorry we screwed up your high school years by fighting all the time' presents."

Her ulterior motive was achieved.

Victor laughed. "Oh man, that sounds like a sweet deal."

"Especially if I asked for something expensive," she said, chuckling. "Then it's a race to see who gets it for me first, and the newest edition."

"I did not realize little Wendy was so conniving," Victor said, turning his head to grin at her.

"I can be," she said. "But I prefer to use my powers for good instead of evil."

Sitting upright, Greg chirped, and pointed out the windshield.

"What? What is it?" Victor asked.

Wendy rolled her eyes. "Greg, seriously?"

He chirped once more, nodding vigorously.

Angling to look past Greg, Wendy said, "He wants to stop for burgers."

Victor took the next exit.

"You got it, bud."

* * * * * * *

"Wendy, please, I'm begging you. Begging. Pleading. On my knees…"

She smirked and turned the volume up. "You already used your song veto for the hour," she said over the music. "Should've chosen more wisely."

Victor groaned. "You've been listening to the same Taylor Swift song on repeat."

"It's Greg's favorite," she countered, glancing back. "Right, Greg?"

Eyes closed, hands folded over his full belly, Greg bobbed his head from side to side as Taylor Swift sang about feeling twenty-two and free. He pulled his thin lips into a smile, opening one eye to look at Wendy.

"Mothman likes T-Swift..." Victor muttered. "They don't mention that in any of the books."

Nodding once at Greg, Wendy waited.

From the backseat, a raspy screeching erupted, scaring Victor so badly he swerved.

"What the—"

Sounding like a stuck pig, Greg continued.

"What's wrong? What's he doing?"

Wendy stared at Victor plainly. "What are you talking about? He's singing."

Victor's jaw fell. "He's..."

"Singing," Wendy repeated. Lowering her voice, she added, "You're not going to make fun of his singing, are you?"

"What? No, I'd never—"

"Don't be mean, Victor," she said. "He's really sensitive about his voice."

Gaping like a fish, Victor looked from Wendy to Greg and then back to the road.

"Uh... No, he sounds amazing," he said, forcing a cheerful tone. "Wow, Greg! You're a natural! You know, if you weren't a super-secret cryptid, I'd say you should go on The Voice or something. You've got the chops, my friend."

Wendy watched with her lips pressed together tightly as Victor attempted to bop along with Greg's screeching.

She had to give him credit, he was *really* trying.

When Greg hit a particularly jarring high note, Victor winced and ducked his head.

She couldn't hold it anymore. Wendy lost it.

Bursting into a fit of laughter, she doubled over.

"He's not singing," she said, breathless and still giggling. "He's just making noise."

"What?"

Greg's noise turned into his wheezing laugh, with delighted chirping punctuating the joke they pulled.

Realization dawned, spreading over Victor's face. "Oh, you're two are hilarious," he said. "Real funny. I was going to go to bat for you, man." He glanced at Greg in the rearview mirror. "You sounded like a dying cat, you know that right?"

Greg chuckled and settled back into his seat, content to *listen* to the music from then on.

* * * * * * *

Wendy zoomed in on the Google Map on her phone, squinting at the road names.

"There's a rest stop just up ahead," she said, gesturing.

"Thank God," Victor sighed. "My bladder is going to burst."

"I told you not to drink the extra-large."

"You know very well my willpower is flimsy at best," he said, passing a particularly slow minivan. Glancing over his shoulder, he asked, "Hey Greg, you need a pitstop?"

An affirmative click gave him an indication, but he still looked to Wendy for confirmation.

"Yes," she said. "Greg, you'll have to be really careful… It looks busy," she added as they pulled into the parking lot.

"Just pull over by that dumpster," Greg clicked, pointing. *"I'll get out."*

Wendy directed Victor and helped Greg maneuver his legs back without kicking anyone in the face.

In a split second, Greg was out of the back seat and awkwardly shuffling behind the large metal dumpsters.

Victor pulled the car into a space nearby and nearly bolted, tossing the keys to Wendy.

"I'll hurry, I promise," he called, jogging towards the men's room.

She shook her head, laughing to herself. She couldn't imagine a goofier scenario.

Walking around to stretch her legs, Wendy rolled her shoulders, easing some of the tension in her back.

The day was surprisingly warm for April, and she was thankful she'd worn denim shorts instead of her original choice of skinny jeans. She didn't know how Victor wasn't dying in his layered tee shirt and plaid overshirt, even if his sleeves were rolled up.

Pulling her thick curls off her neck, Wendy tilted her face up at the bright noonday sky and closed her eyes.

When was the last time she'd simply relaxed and enjoyed the day?

Wendy made a mental note to study outside more. If it didn't help her GPA maybe it would benefit her complexion.

Footsteps announced Victor's return, and she blinked her eyes open.

"Sorry, didn't mean to interrupt your moment of Zen," he said, smiling softly.

"You didn't," she told him, letting her hair fall down her back once more.

Holding up two plastic candy packages, he asked, "M&Ms or Reese's Pieces?"

"Reese's, duh."

"Of course."

Just as they were about to open their candy, a woman's scream wrenched their heads around.

"A bear!" She shrieked. Dropping what looked like empty fast-food containers, she ran away. "A bear!"

Wendy and Victor stared at each other in panic.

"Greg," they said in unison.

Rushing back to the car, they spotted Greg's dark head peering out from behind the dumpster.

"Greg," Wendy whispered harshly. "C'mon!"

Victor flung open the back door before climbing into the driver's seat, turning the engine. Greg leapt into the back, rocking the car with the force of his landing.

"Go, go, go," Wendy urged.

"I'm going, I'm going!"

Peeling out of the parking lot, they struggled to buckle their seatbelts while frantically avoiding anyone noticing them or seeing inside.

No one said anything until they were on the highway again.

Victor laughed first. "I think you took five years off that soccer mom's life."

Sitting up as far as he could, Greg leaned forward between the two seats. Looking remorsefully at Wendy, he clicked.

"It's okay, Greg," she said with a chuckle. "No harm, no foul."

Chapter Twelve

May 18th, 2015

Wendy crossed her arms as she approached Greg's latest favorite tree.

"Greg, you up there?"

She squinted through the darkness, trying to decipher his shape in the branches.

"What are you doing here?" He clicked, rustling the leaves as he moved. **"I thought you were going to… Um, what's it called?"**

"Prom," she said, word dropping like a stone out of her mouth.

"Right. I thought you were going to prom."

Wendy scowled. "I was, but…" She shook her head. "Can you just come down here?"

In an instant, Greg glided out of the tree and swooped down to the ground below.

"What's wrong?" He chirped gently.

"I've officially become a cliché," she said, attempting to laugh. "My date stood me up."

"The boy from your English class?"

"That's the one."

Staring down at her shoes, she focused on the tuft of grass near the toe. Imagined it was Trey's face as she squashed it.

"I thought he liked you."

She choked on a laugh. "I thought so too."

Dropping into a crouch, Greg looked up at her. **"Is this how people treat someone they like?"**

"No. Well, they're not supposed to, anyway."

Greg was quiet, red eyes blinking in the dark.

"Where's prom?"

Wendy frowned. "The school gym."

In the faint light from the moon, she saw the tips of his teeth as he grinned. **"I have an idea."**

Ten minutes and a very cramped car ride later, Wendy was certain she was going to throw up.

This was such a bad idea.

Squatting behind a Ford truck she was pretty sure belonged to one of the basketball players, she and Greg waited.

"That one?" *He clicked.*

"No, that's my lab partner. He's nice."

Greg nodded. **"Is it him?"**

"Who—Greg, that's my P.E. teacher." She swatted his arm.

"You don't like P.E. either…"

"Please don't."

"Fine…"

She was just about to force him to abort his half-baked mission, when a familiar car drove up. A simple blue Mazda with a bunch of John Deere bumper stickers on the back.

Wendy gasped and Greg arched his neck to see.

"Him?"

She covered her mouth and nodded.

Greg's wheezing laugh had never seemed so menacing until that moment.

"Greg, maybe you shouldn't…" She whispered, clutching his shoulder.

Red eyes narrowed at her. ***"He hurt your feelings,"*** *he grunted, and before she could argue, Greg was crawling out from behind the truck.*

She watched with her heart in her throat as Greg scurried along the ground like an oversized lizard towards the Mazda.

Trey and his new date were still in the car, silhouetted by the parking lot lights.

From what Wendy could see they were kissing—or more accurately, trying to climb into each other's mouths—totally unaware of the dark figure climbing up the back of the car, over the trunk, and onto the roof.

The car rocked from Greg's weight, and an alarmed shriek could be heard even with the windows rolled up.

Wendy had to give Greg credit. Theatrics came naturally to him.

He waited, giving them time to talk themselves down. She could see their pantomiming as they convinced each other it was fine.

It was probably nothing... They couldn't see anything, so it must have been someone walking by...

Greg inched up to the edge of the windshield, planting his huge hands on the glass first before dropping his head upside-down and baring his teeth.

The screams were jarring even from a distance.

Wendy jumped, clasping her hand over her mouth to stop from laughing.

Swinging over the windshield, Greg landed on the front hood, talons gouging metal as he perched himself. Cocking his head, he stared into the car at the terrified couple flailing around before screeching at them and leaning on the glass.

Trey clamored to start the car, but his keys went flying, dropping somewhere in the floorboards.

Wendy laughed, clutching her belly as tears sprang to her eyes.

With one last high-pitched yell, Greg flapped his wings aggressively and shook the car as he took off into the dark.

Seconds later, Trey and his date—Marissa, from their second period physics class—bolted from the car, screaming for help, that Mothman had just tried to attack them.

"Get away from me," Marissa shouted at Trey as he tried to comfort her. "I knew this was a bad idea—don't touch me!"

A small group of seniors ran over, inspecting the hood of the Mazda and trying not to snicker at the huge wet spot on the front of Trey's suit pants.

Wendy had to prop herself up on the truck wheel as she laughed until her ribs ached.

The gravel behind her shifted and she turned to look.

"How was that?" *Greg clicked, dark eyebrows lifted in glee.*

"You were right," she wheezed. "That was a great idea."

* * * * * * *

An hour outside the city, Victor bemoaned they needed to stop for gas.

Choosing the station that was across from a Starbucks was for Wendy's benefit. If she didn't get more caffeine in her system soon, she'd be passing out before they even made it to Pittsburg.

Maybe she *was* a little too heavily addicted to caffeine…

Not that she'd be trying to get off it that weekend.

As Victor took the exit, Wendy turned in her seat to help Greg cover himself with a blanket.

"Can I get coffee too?" He chirped, tugging on the corners of the fabric.

"Greg, you know what happened last time you had caffeine."

He grunted, pulling his long legs up to his chest so he'd fit under the cheap Wal-Mart throw. *"But that was years ago. I'm sure I'm fine now."*

Victor frowned. "Greg isn't allowed to have coffee?"

"He reacts… poorly," she sighed, tucking the sides in by Greg's knees.

"I can handle it now, I promise," Greg clicked. His head was completely covered, leaving him a shapeless blob filling the entire backseat.

Wendy continued to tell him no, absolutely not, as Victor pulled next to a pump.

"Just stay here, Greg, okay?" She said as she got out. "I'll bring you back a cake-pop."

His chirp was muffled as she closed the door.

Wendy was several paces away when she heard Victor open the door again and whisper, "What about a Frappuccino?"

Rolling her eyes, she groaned. She didn't have the artificial energy for this.

The Starbucks was about as busy as expected for a mid-day rush.

Making her way past several clusters of people to stand in line, she glanced up at the menu, wondering if adding an extra shot of espresso would help or send her into a caffeine induced panic attack.

Wendy frowned. She should at least *attempt* not to seem like she was purposefully giving herself an ulcer.

She was still getting a large though. With extra syrup.

As the line moved, she stepped in front of the baked goods display case, hovering over the pastries. Too busy weighing her cake-pop options, she didn't notice Victor at all.

Not until he came up behind her, bumping her with his elbow.

"You going to tell me what the deal with coffee is?"

She smirked, still looking at the multi-colored desserts. "Imagine the most hyperactive child you've ever seen. I'm talking screaming, running, jumping, the whole nine yards. Now give him wings and talons and make him a creature people aren't supposed to know exists."

Victor paled. "I'll make his Frappuccino decaf."

"Good call."

As they got up to the register to order, Victor cursed under his breath.

"No... No, no, no..." He turned away, scrubbing a hand over his jaw. "How? How is this happening?"

Caught off guard, Wendy forgot to ask for the extra syrup before the barista wandered away.

Concerned, she frowned at him. "What?"

Victor scratched the back of his neck. "Uh... My ex is here."

Wendy nearly gave herself whiplash.

"What?" She asked, a little too loudly, wrenching her neck to see.

"Shh, don't make it obvious," he pleaded, trying to hide behind a rack of seasonal coffee blends.

She was at a loss. She couldn't see anyone in the café who looked like someone Victor would date.

"Sorry, where?"

He busied himself by pretending to read the description on the Sumatran whole bean.

"Near the front. The brunette in the pink shorts."

Wendy stalled.

Oh.

She vaguely knew the girl from school—had seen her around campus. They had a lecture class together last semester. Wendy remembered the girl's ever-present high ponytail swish-swishing along the chairback from the row in front of her.

"Her?" She said and regretted her tone immediately. "I meant... Not that you... She's just—"

"Too good for me?" He supplied, still staring at the same label. "Trust me, I know."

Wendy shook her head. "That's not what I was going to say. She just seems a little... white bread for you."

"She's pre-law," he said. Hazarding a glance up, he arched his neck to look over the heads of the people in front of them. "White-bread is going to make her a millionaire one day."

Mulling over his words, Wendy chewed the inside of her bottom lip.

Victor had never told her he was seeing someone, or more accurately, *had been* seeing someone. She knew he had dated casually, had even helped him pick the least obnoxious shirts to wear and offered alternative places to meet than just the Student Union or the café attached to the library.

But he'd never mentioned dating someone seriously or long enough to become an ex later on.

Never told her about a heart-wrenching breakup.

"When did you two date?" Wendy asked, crossing her arms.

"Last year."

"For how long?"

Victor flushed, ducking his head once more. "Um… About, I don't know… Like, six months?"

"You were dating her six months and never told me about her?" Wendy asked under her breath.

The pink tinting his cheeks and ears deepened. "We were kind of keeping it… on the DL."

"You?" She scoffed. "Mister can't keep a secret? Mister 'I have to announce every life event as soon as I walk into a room'? You were keeping a six-month relationship on the down-low?"

Shame darkened Victor's eyes as he pressed his lips together tightly.

Wendy's stomach dropped.

Oh…

"It wasn't your idea, was it?" She whispered.

Victor shrugged, tucking his hands into his pockets. "For the record, I *can* keep a secret. And she just didn't think her friends would… Understand, I guess."

"Understand what?" Wendy turned to glare at the back of the pretty brunette's head. "That you're not some Ken doll that matches her Pinterest perfect five-year plan?"

"I don't know if she'd use those exact words, but…"

She sneered. "What a bitch."

"Wendy."

Facing him, she caught his stare. "She hid you like some dirty little secret," she snapped, barely keeping her voice down. "You're not the one who should be hiding in embarrassment here."

"I am not hiding…"

"You turned yourself into a contortionist to keep her from seeing you," she said.

He angled to look around her surreptitiously. "I… I was just…"

Wendy couldn't take it anymore.

Grabbing his hand, she dragged him towards the drink pick-up counter, in direct line of vision of his ex.

Standing tall, Wendy pressed the heels of her palms onto the counter and leaned back.

Victor acted like he was going to have a stroke.

Then the girl glanced up from her phone and Wendy knew what a true cardiac episode looked like. She was surprised her perfect ponytail didn't curl at the ends.

Waving awkwardly, Victor attempted a smile. "H-hey, Heather."

"Victor…" She blinked at him. "I, uh… What a surprise."

"Yeah, we're, um… Going to that symposium thing for Doctor Brown's class," he said, gesturing to Wendy.

"So am I," Heather said, nodding. "I didn't know you cared about political writing so much."

Victor's nervous flush returned. "Well, it was kind of…"

"He wanted to come with me," Wendy interjected.

In that moment, she was convinced she'd lost her mind.

But that revelation didn't stop her from continuing.

Staring up at Victor, she batted her eyelashes and added, "He's keeping me company for the weekend."

With bulging eyes, Victor nodded slowly.

"Oh, that's…" Heather looked from Victor to Wendy. "Sweet."

Looping her arm through the crook of his elbow, Wendy grinned. "Isn't it? He's the best."

As Victor tried to gather his jaw off the floor, Wendy gave Heather a cold once over.

"Sorry, I'm not sure he's mentioned you," she said. "You are…?"

"Heather," she said, tone deadening.

Just as Wendy flashed a big, 'I'll eat you alive' smile, their order was called, and she patted Victor on the chest.

"Guess that's us. It was nice to meet you, *Hilary*." She enjoyed the outraged expression at her purposeful misnaming. "Enjoy the symposium."

With a face reminiscent of curdled milk, Heather watched them gather their drinks and stroll away.

Victor hurried to keep up as Wendy left the building.

"I can't believe you did that!" He exclaimed, balancing a drink tray and grinning as he looked over his shoulder.

"She deserved it," Wendy said as they crossed the street. "And I'd do it again in a heartbeat. The nerve of her…"

When they got to the car, Victor set the drinks on the hood and dug out his keys.

"You're possibly the most wicked and conniving person I've ever known, and I *love* it. I'm now infinitely more terrified of you, but I love it."

A sudden, potent protectiveness flooded Wendy's system.

"She treated you like garbage, Victor. Dated you for six months and never once let you be public with it. No one, *especially* you, should ever be made to feel like an embarrassment." She yanked open the passenger side door. "You're too good for that."

Climbing into the car, she buckled her seatbelt before taking the drink tray from him.

A small grin tugged at the corner of Victor's mouth. "Especially me, huh?"

Wendy didn't miss a beat. "Especially you."

Muffled chirps brought both their heads around.

"Oh, hang on, Greg," she told him, pulling his Frappuccino free from the tray. "Geez, what is this?"

"Double mocha chip with extra whip cream, extra chocolate sauce, and sugar sprinkles," Victor said.

Wendy grimaced. "I feel sick just looking at it."

Tugging the blanket off just enough to get his arm out, Greg took it from her and clicked happily.

"You're welcome," Victor said, beaming. Then he blinked and looked to Wendy. "Oh my God, I think I understood him."

"He said add caramel next time."

Victor's face fell. "Really?"

"No," Wendy laughed. "He said thank you."

Shaking his head at her, Victor pulled back out onto the street. "Tricky, wicked, conniving woman."

* * * * * * *

They were so close to Pittsburgh Wendy could barely contain her nervous fidgeting every time they passed a mile marker sign.

She knew she shouldn't put too much faith in finding other Mothmen in one weekend, but she couldn't help it. The answers about Greg's past were tantalizingly within reach, and even if he wouldn't admit it, she knew he was just as excited about the possibilities.

Over the music, rapid thudding jarred Wendy from her thoughts.

"Vic, what's that?"

He scowled, gripping the wheel tighter. "Uh… I'm not sure."

Thwap thwap thwap.

The car slowed as he eased off the accelerator.

"Victor?" Wendy turned in her seat, staring first at him then out the back windshield.

"I think we have a flat tire," he said, already pulling off the highway onto the shoulder.

"Oh no… Seriously?"

Distracted from his bag of potato chips, Greg lifted his gaze. *"Is that bad?"*

"Sort of," she answered. "It'll just delay us for a bit."

Parking a safe distance away from the lanes of traffic, Victor turned off the ignition. "Don't worry, I've got a spare."

"Do you have a jack?" Wendy asked.

Victor rolled his eyes at her. "Do I have a jack…" He scoffed, opening his door.

Watching from his reclined position in the back, Greg tugged at the blanket draped across his middle and settled in. *"This is going to take a while, isn't it?"*

"Probably," Wendy sighed. Unbuckling her seatbelt, she moved to get out. "Stay here, Greg. I'll be right back."

He chirped an affirmative before shoving his face into the plastic *Lays* bag, scarfing up every last crumb.

The whirring buzz of hunks of metal going seventy miles an hour set Wendy's teeth on edge. Her uncle was a state patrolman; she was acutely aware of the danger they were in.

Circling around to the trunk, she yanked her plaid overshirt off, tying it around her waist. No sense in getting more than her bare arms dirty.

"Okay, so, good news and bad news," Victor said as she approached. "Bad news is, the spare tire is flat."

Wendy groaned. "Are you kidding me, Vic?"

He waved a hand out. "But the good news is, I have triple A!"

Victor was not an idiot. Wendy knew that. But he was clearly struggling to put a few more pieces together.

"Uh huh," she said, crossing her arms. "And what exactly do you plan on telling the nice road side repair guy when he sees the eight foot tall cryptid in your back seat?"

Victor's face fell. "Oh."

"Yeah. *Oh*."

Gesturing frantically, he cried, "Okay, but what else are we supposed to do? Hitch hike to Pittsburg? Can't do that with a cryptid either."

"Shhh." Wendy took a step closer, pressing her finger to her lips.

Victor squinted at her. "Who exactly can hear me right now?" He glanced over his shoulder at the speeding traffic. "God? Pretty sure if the almighty exists, he knows about Greg."

Grabbing him by the shoulder, she spun him around to see the work crew digging along the median. Several burly men in orange reflective vests had stopped what they were doing, watching the two and their broken-down car with interest.

"Oh no," Victor muttered, tugging at the ends of his brown hair.

"Just ignore them," Wendy told him, yanking on his shirt sleeve. "Pretend you're capable of handling this situation."

"I thought we just established I'm *not* capable of handling this situation."

"Victor."

Puffing his cheeks out like a blowfish, he stooped over the open trunk and exhaled noisily.

"I still can't do anything about the flat tire. Well, the two flat tires."

Looking over his shoulder, she asked, "The spare is just low on air, right? So if we can get it to a pump, we'll be fine."

"You want to carry a tire three miles to the nearest gas station?"

Wendy sighed. "If it's our only option…"

Straightening abruptly, Victor knocked into her, nearly headbutting her.

"Whoa, I'm—"

"Ow! Really, Victor?"

"I'm sorry, I didn't see you!"

"Hey!"

They both froze, registering the voice was directed at them.

"Hey, y'all need help?"

Still rubbing the sore spot in her collar bone, Wendy stepped to the side to see one of the workmen waving at them. The traffic wasn't as thick, and she could tell he was contemplating jogging across the lanes to join them.

"Oh, no, that's okay," she called back. "We're sorting it out."

Taking his helmet off and handing it to his buddy, the man gauged the oncoming cars like an Olympian eyeing the fifty-meter pole vault.

"Shit, he's coming over," she whispered. "Hide Greg."

Victor stared at her, flabbergasted. "Do *what* now?"

Pushing the trunk lid up further to hide the back windshield, Wendy urged him again to do something.

As the construction worker started his way across, Victor panicked, flailing like an electroshocked deer.

"Oh God, oh God," he muttered, spinning in a circle before finally leaping around the corner of the trunk and sliding along the metal until he stopped directly in front of the passenger window.

"Hey," the man greeted, waving to both of them as he finished crossing the road. "Flat tire, huh?"

Wendy smiled, hoping it looked natural and not at all freaked out or petrified.

"Yeah, and our spare's low on air. We were just going to take it to a gas station to fill it."

The closer he got, Wendy could see he wasn't much older than they were. Maybe twenty-two or twenty-three if she had to guess. He was covered in a thin sheen of sweat and dust, but that didn't detract from his handsome features and bright blue eyes.

She made a concerted effort not to ogle his well-muscled frame, no matter how much he looked like one of the stars on those teen soap opera style shows her cousins loved to watch.

Victor simply jerked his chin at the guy, crossing his arms as he leaned back impossibly far to cover the window.

"Nearest gas station is a ways down the road," the newcomer said. Glancing at Victor, he asked, "You got triple A?"

Turning slightly to face him, Victor opened his mouth to speak, but Wendy cut him off.

"No. He doesn't."

The glare Victor shot her over the guy's shoulder was comically exaggerated, but still made her wince.

A Greyhound bus drove by, hydraulics hissing as if scolding her for what she'd metaphorically done.

Stand up for Victor one minute, undercut him the next. No wonder he was still eyeing her like she'd just spat in his face.

Scared desperation was an ugly look on anyone, and Wendy was starting to feel it too.

Wiping his hand on his jeans, the guy extended it in greeting. "I'm Derek."

"Wendy," she answered, noting the callouses on his palm. "And this is Victor."

Giving a short wave, Victor returned to sulking in the background.

"Mind if I take a look?" Derek asked.

"Sure," she told him, stepping to the side so he could see the pitiful spare in the trunk.

After a few moments, Derek hummed under his breath and tilted his head.

"We've got an air pump in the truck that might fit this," he said. "Could give it a shot. Would save you the trek to the Shell station."

"Oh my God, really?" Wendy only realized afterwards how the amount of glee in her voice could be interpreted, but at that point she didn't care. If he had a way to get them out of there, she'd take it.

Derek smiled, and oh—oh wow.

Stunning didn't begin to cover it.

"Absolutely." Hoisting the tire out, Derek nodded. "Give me a couple minutes and we'll get you sorted." He started towards the road and glanced over his shoulder. "Don't go anywhere."

Wendy chuckled at his corny joke.

Clearing her throat, she tried to appear casual as he walked away.

When he was out of ear shot, Victor sighed like a disgruntled child.

"What?"

"Nothing," he muttered. "Thanks for having my back, by the way."

"Oh, come on, Vic," she groaned. "If we'd said yes, he just would have suggested we call and we already know why we can't do that."

"No, of course not, you'd just rather make me a human shield while you make goo-goo eyes at the hot construction guy. I get it."

"I didn't call him over here," she said, flushing with anger.

He refused to look at her, glowering into the distance as he spoke. "Didn't have to accept his help either."

Wendy inhaled, ready to launch into a withering dismantling of Victor's argument, when there was a tap at the back windshield that made them both turn around.

"Can I crack a window?" Greg chirped, voice muffled by the glass.

"No, Greg," she told him.

Two muddy red eyes peered out from the gap of the trunk. *"But it's stuffy in here."*

"We're almost done."

The high-pitched trill was his version of a whine, and Wendy rolled her eyes so far back she gave herself a headache.

Now she had *two* grumpy, pouting boys on her hands. Great.

"You're both insufferable," she said, sitting on the bumper to continue waiting.

As she stared at the dirt between her feet, she listened to Victor's shoulders squeak against the car each time he shifted.

"How long does it take to fill a tire?" He mumbled, refolding his arms.

Wendy pushed her hair out of her face. "Could you be a little more grateful? He's helping us."

Twisting to look at her, he said, "He's flirting with you."

"So?"

She felt like a middle schooler again—defiant lip curl twisting across her face as she glared over her shoulder.

Victor's eyes widened. "*So?*"

"So what if he's flirting with me," she said. "It's not totally out of the question someone might think I'm attractive."

"I didn't mean… It's just—" Shoving his hand through his hair, he chewed on the last few sounds at the back of his throat.

Wendy scowled.

What were they even arguing about?

"It doesn't matter either way," she continued. "Once he's done, we'll put the tire back on the car and be out of here in twenty minutes."

"Oh, I get it…" Victor drawled, rolling his neck. "It's just part of your schtick."

"Excuse me?"

"Modus operandi Wendy," he muttered. "Play along to get what you need, then bail."

His words knocked the air from her lungs.

She'd never known Victor to be cruel, but she guessed there was a first time for everything.

"Is that what you think of me?" She said, barely audible through the lump in her throat. "That I'm some cold-hearted manipulator?"

The cloud of bitter jealousy surrounding Victor began to dissipate.

"Wen—"

"Don't talk to me," she snapped, turning away from him. "There's nothing you could say that I'd want to hear right now."

"Hey," he started, already stepping around the back of the car. "I didn't mean—"

From the other side of the highway, Derek called out. "Good to go now!"

Victor retreated to his station at the window, crossing his arms once more.

Standing, Wendy brushed the dust off her hands and forced a smile.

"Sounds great," she shouted over the noise of the speeding cars.

Derek waited for the next break in traffic before rolling the tire across, jogging next to it. He grinned as he delivered it to her, all but ignoring Victor.

"She'll get you where you need to go now," he said, leaning the spare against the bumper. "You know a good garage to patch the other one?"

Tucking a thick lock of curls behind her ear, she glanced from the tire back to Derek. "Oh, uh… yeah, we've got someone. Thanks."

"Not a problem." Hovering a moment, Derek looked over to Victor's stoic profile. "You need a hand with the jack?"

"Nope. Got it covered." Victor didn't even turn to speak to him.

"You sure? I don't mind."

"Oh yeah. I'm sure."

Derek turned to Wendy ruefully. "Alright, well... If you change your mind, just holler."

"Thank you," Wendy said before Victor could rudely dismiss him once more.

Adjusting the tire on the bumper again, he squinted over the trunk lid at the windshield and paused.

"Is there someone else in the—"

Lurching ungracefully in front of him, Wendy plastered a smile wider than the Ohio river across her face. "Thanks so much again for your help," she said, a few octaves higher than usual.

Startled, he pointed behind her. "It looked like—"

"Have a good one!" She exclaimed, practically forcing him back with sheer willpower.

Wendy couldn't have been happier to be a stranger in that town, never to see this man again.

Derek furrowed his sweaty brow but didn't argue. "Yeah, uh... you too."

He made it to the middle of the lanes before Victor lost the battle against his laughing fit.

Rolling the tire over to his side, she muttered, "Still think I'm black widow in training?"

Victor's amusement vanished. "Hey, about that…"

"I don't want to talk about it."

He reached for her but pulled up short.

"No, really," he continued. "It was…" He sighed. "I didn't mean to be that…"

Wendy glared at him. "Nasty?"

He nodded. "Yeah, let's go with that."

Crossing her arms over her stomach, Wendy stared out at the field to their right.

"I guess the truth comes out eventually," she said, about to walk away.

Victor scrambled to keep the tire from rolling away as he stepped closer. "But it's not," he said. "I just… I let my ego get the best of me."

Frowning, Wendy asked, "You're blaming this on being jealous?"

A flush spread rapidly up Victor's cheeks as he snorted, rolling his eyes.

"I was not jealous."

Realization dawned on her and Wendy fought to hide her smirk. "Oh my God, you totally were."

"Nuh-uhh," he mumbled, squatting down to slide the jack into place.

"You were a jealous, mouthy jerk," she said. "And you can't even admit it."

As he worked, Victor glanced up. "I admit I was a jerk, and I'm always mouthy. But why would I be jealous of that guy?"

Wendy leaned against the side of the car. "I don't know, Vic. You tell me."

Victor's grip slid from the wrench, causing his elbow to smack into the metal with a sharp clang. Hissing in pain, he grabbed his arm and let out a string of inventive curses.

"Looks like you've got it covered here," she said primly, tucking her hands into her pockets. "I'll leave you to it."

Another tap at the back window caught her attention.

Greg's muffled clicking was barely audible over the traffic noise.

"Now can I open a window?"

Chapter Thirteen

Crossing into the city should have felt momentous.

A milestone reached in their search for the other Mothmen. At least that's what Wendy had expected.

Truthfully it felt just like passing any other city limit—silent, maybe a little bumpy, and totally mundane.

Afternoon sun still blazed through the windshield, limiting their abilities to search for any possible cryptids, so they did the next best thing.

Greg sat forward between the front seats, staring intently out the front of the car as they drove along the Fort Pitt Bridge. The small, dark points of cartilage that gave shape to his inhuman ears twitched and swiveled like satellite dishes.

"Do you notice anything different? Unusual?" Wendy asked, glancing at him.

"No," he clicked. *"It just looks like a bridge…"*

"Do you hear anything?"

Greg paused. *"Not yet."*

Victor cast a look at Wendy, asking, "Hey, can he feel stuff—like that psychic feeling you told me about before?"

"Greg's not psychic," she sighed.

"I might be," Greg countered with a shrug.

"Being psychic means you predict things that are going to happen." Wendy shifted in her seat so she didn't have to twist her neck uncomfortably. "Does that sound like you?"

Greg's eyebrows knitted together in a deep frown. She'd never seen him so suddenly troubled before.

"Maybe," he grunted, barely loud enough to hear over the noise of the car.

Before she could question him further, Victor interrupted.

"So, psychic label aside, if Greg could sense danger, that means the other Moth-kin probably can too, right? Like, it's a species thing, not just a Greg thing."

"I guess so," Wendy said, looking over her shoulder. "What do you think?"

Greg nodded. *"I don't think it's just me."*

Looking in the rearview, Victor addressed Greg. "The Moth-kin spotted in Pittsburg were on this bridge. Do you think they were trying to warn people about it?"

Greg's ears swiveled once more as he thought over the question. *"I don't feel anything wrong with the bridge but... They must be trying to warn people about something."*

"Must be?" Victor asked once Wendy translated.

"It's an instinct, of sorts," Greg clicked. *"To try to communicate, to make people understand. Maybe that's just*

how it is for me because of my accident, but it's a powerful urge. To want to help in some way."

Wendy translated again and Victor frowned. "Like the Silver Bridge collapse," he said.

Sorrow pulled at Greg's features, and he stared down at his clawed hands. *"Yes."*

"Greg, what aren't you telling me about the bridge collapse?" Wendy asked, turning almost completely around in her seat to look at him. "You always told me you knew something bad was going to happen, but you never said you knew the specifics."

"I didn't, at first," he clicked. *"But then I could hear it... Like an echo. I could hear cars, and metal, and..."* He trailed off, shaking his head.

"You never told me that," Wendy murmured, reaching for his hand.

Adjusting his grip on the wheel, Victor said, "People blamed you for the collapse, but you were never there."

"I was on the river bank," Greg explained, waiting for Wendy to relay his words. *"I knew, and I couldn't stop it. Couldn't find the origin point of the sound. I don't blame people for thinking it was my fault."*

"Greg, there was nothing you could have done," Wendy said.

"Doesn't take the pain away though," he chirped quietly.

As the silence stretched, Victor sat up ramrod straight, suddenly anxious.

"Guys, if Moth-folk make themselves known as a warning, and this bridge seems fine..." He glanced at Wendy before looking in the rearview. "Then what the hell are the others trying to warn people about?"

Greg and Wendy stared at each other, their hands clutched tight.

"Victor," she said. "We need a map."

* * * * * * *

Checking into the cheap motor lodge on the other side of the city hadn't been difficult at all.

Getting Greg out of the car without making a scene, however, took some intense look-out signals, acrobatics, and a spontaneous addition of a baggage cart. Once on the rickety metal device, Victor covered Greg with a blanket like he was a monk hunched over in contrition and wheeled him into the room while Wendy gathered their things.

They didn't waste any time.

As soon as their bags were dropped unceremoniously on the floor, Victor dug out the map he'd been using to mark possible Mothmen hiding spots, and unfolded it across one of the beds.

"Okay, so, if Moth-kin are out here trying to warn the people of Pittsburg about a disaster, where would that disaster take place?"

With hands on his hips Victor stared at Greg, who only looked up from where he was crouched in confusion.

"Don't ask me," he clicked. *"It's not like I'm that familiar with the city."*

"I think he's asking for hints," Wendy said. "Like, where would be the most likely place another Mothman would sense danger?"

"That's still awfully vague."

"Okay, well you could try to narrow it—"

"You're asking an amnesiac to become an expert all of a sudden?"

Crossing her arms, Wendy assessed Greg with a sharp gaze.

Turning on her heels, she strode over to their pile of belongings and rummaged around for a moment. Returning with something in each hand, she held out a package of Twinkies and the bottle of barbeque sauce.

"Have a snack, Greg," she said sweetly.

"I'm not grumpy…" He clicked, but took the food from her anyway, opening the plastic and taking a huge bite.

Leaning over to Victor, she whispered, "Give him a couple minutes."

Sure enough, after the Twinkies had been demolished, and Greg had licked all the sauce and cream filling off his talons, he turned back to the map with enthusiasm.

"I don't know exactly where they'd be sensing danger, or why, but I know what happened with me before the bridge collapse. It was mostly sounds—though I didn't recognize them—and the feeling."

"The dread?" Wendy asked.

Greg shook his head. *"The vibration."*

When Wendy translated, Victor's eyes grew wide.

"The bridge, your car..." He started jotting notes on the motel stationary. "Maybe it has to do with metal."

"Metal?"

"Yeah, maybe he can sense the vibration changes. Or even hear them," he said, going to stand next to Greg, peering into his ear opening. "How good is your hearing, anyway?"

Blinking at Victor, Greg arched an eyebrow. *"Better than yours, I bet."*

Wendy smirked, paraphrasing in her translation. "It's good."

"So, then that's probably what it is," Victor said. "He's hearing or sensing the change in pitch of vibrations through metal."

"That doesn't exactly narrow down our choices, Victor," Wendy said, gesturing to the map. "In case you haven't noticed, the whole city is made of metal."

Scratching the back of his neck, Victor groaned. "Yeah, that's… a lot of ground to cover."

After a beat, he looked to Greg once more, grinning broadly.

"But we know someone with wings and supernatural abilities to literally sense impending danger."

Greg glanced from Victor to Wendy and back to Victor.

"Okay."

"It's risky," Wendy said at the same time. "Greg, are you sure?"

"Maybe I can look for the others too," he clicked, leaning over to stare at the map closely. *"If they're out there, I bet I can find them."*

Wendy's chest constricted, forcing her to take only shallow breaths.

She already hated this plan.

"Wendy?" Victor asked, yanking her out of her imminent panic spiral.

"Alright," she relented. "I guess we just have to wait for nightfall."

Victor sprinted to the TV stand, grabbing the remote. "Dibs!"

"Not fair."

He didn't need a translation for Greg's disappointed pouting.

* * * * * * *

There were only so many episodes of *Unsolved Mysteries* Wendy could take before she thought she was going to lose it.

Not that she disliked the show, but Victor's constant commentary and additional theories were driving her nuts.

Greg, however, enjoyed it all immensely.

"How does someone jump from a plane and not be found?" He clicked, pantomiming to help Victor understand him. *"Weren't people looking for him?"*

"No one knows," Victor said. "That's the unsolved part of the mystery. Most people think he died, and his body was never recovered. Personally, I think he survived and changed his identity and just started a new life."

"People do that?"

Victor furrowed his brow, trying to follow. "I… Yeah, I guess so."

Tossing the two-year-old *Us Weekly* she'd been reading onto the bed, Wendy sighed and stood up.

"I'm getting dinner," she said, grabbing a copy of the room key and her wallet. "Everyone good with diner food?"

She knew Greg would never say no to pancakes and hash browns.

"Sure," both Victor and Greg said at the same time.

They both looked like little kids sitting cross-legged, eyes glued to the television. Wendy smiled, taken with how sweet it was.

Of course, Greg chose that moment to burp so loudly it reverberated off the walls. As Victor laughed, Wendy rolled her eyes.

"I'll be back."

The diner was only around the block, and surprisingly fast for a to-go order of that size.

Wendy knew better than to skimp on food for Greg, otherwise he'd be eating her dinner too.

Balancing the tower of Styrofoam containers, she headed back for the room, praying she didn't turn into a slapstick routine on the way.

"Nice and easy," she muttered to herself as she navigated the curb. "Nice... and... easy."

"Hey," Victor called, coming around the corner. "I was hoping to catch you."

Wendy stopped. "Is everything okay?"

"Oh, yeah, I just belatedly realized 'dinner' for Greg would be about a metric ton of food, and that you'd probably need help," he said, reaching for the boxes on top of the stack.

Grateful for the load to be lifted, she smiled. "Thanks. You didn't have to do that though."

"Are you kidding?" He adjusted his grip on the containers. "My mom would ring my neck if she found out I was that much of a lazy jerk."

"Your mom sounds like my dad."

Walking back towards the room, Wendy glanced up at Victor, taking note of his unruly brown hair and the slight five-o'clock shadow along his jawline.

Only he could make disheveled look… Well, cute.

"Don't say it," he groaned, and Wendy jumped slightly.

"Say what?"

"I know I need a haircut," he said. "It's getting too long. I'm starting to look like the guy from *Ancient Aliens*."

"I don't know, I kind of like it."

Wendy immediately wanted to swallow her own tongue.

Her cheeks burned like she'd forgotten sunscreen while at the lake.

She was never more grateful for her long curly mane of hair she could hide behind.

Victor stared at her for a beat longer than usual. "You do?"

"I…"

Wendy looked up, struggling to find the words, only to see the door to their motel room propped open and a maid cart parked outside.

"Victor. Did you put the 'do not disturb' sign on the door?"

"Um…"

"*Victor.*"

Taking off at a jog, she miraculously held onto the food without dropping a single container. Shouldering the door open further, she skidded to a halt, startling the housekeeper who was vacuuming.

"Oh goodness," The middle-aged woman gasped and then chuckled, turning the Hoover off. "Sorry, dear. I'll only be a moment."

Running in behind her, Victor nearly knocked Wendy over.

Mumbling an apology, he stared in wide-eyed horror as they both scanned the room.

The television was still on, as was the lamp by Victor's bed.

But there was no sign of Greg.

Leaning in close to Wendy's ear, Victor whispered, "Where did he go?"

"I don't know," she murmured back. Setting the food down, she glanced at him. "Just... act natural."

"Do you two have enough pillows?" The housekeeper asked, emptying the minimal trash they'd amassed.

"Yes, ma'am," Wendy said, craning her neck to look in the far corner.

Where the hell was he?

He was a cryptid, not a phantom. He couldn't just vanish...

When she turned to face Victor, he was stock still and pale, staring at her like he'd seen a ghost.

'What?' she mouthed, and he pointed up with one index finger.

Slowly, Wendy tilted her head.

There, clinging to the ceiling with all fours like a mutant gecko, was Greg.

His wings tucked against his body tightly, he crept from the main room towards the bathroom without making a sound.

Wendy wondered absently if a twenty-one-year-old could have a fatal heart attack from shock, or if that was only for elderly people.

Swaying a little, she tried to school her expression as the woman moved around the suite.

Victor grabbed Wendy's wrist, squeezing reassuringly.

The housekeeper clearly hadn't seen Greg. It was at least a partial win.

Just as he slipped into the bathroom, the woman returned with a stack of towels and wash cloths.

"I'll just put these away for you," she said with a smile, striding past them.

Wendy and Victor both stammered, trying desperately to convince her she didn't have to, but it was too late.

Unable to stop herself, Wendy followed, ready to distract the woman by any means necessary. She wasn't above faking a fainting spell.

But when she got to the doorway and looked up, Greg was nowhere to be seen.

"Do you need extra shampoo?" The housekeeper asked, glancing at Wendy's curls with a slight grin on her face.

"No, thank you," she said, twisting around to see where Greg could have possibly tucked himself away.

Wendy did a double take.

The shower curtain had been pulled closed, when she distinctly remembered Victor yanking it back as they'd settled into the room, saying something about checking for serial killers.

Leaning back a fraction, Wendy peered into the shower between the gap in the wall and the curtain.

There, squished in an uncomfortable looking position at the bottom of the tub, was Greg blinking up at her.

The poor guy looked just as spooked as she felt.

"Alright you two," the woman said, walking back out through the room to her cart. "If you need anything else, just call the front desk. Have a great night."

"Thank you very much," Victor said, hurrying to close the door behind her. As soon as the lock clicked, he slumped against it, sighing all the air out of his lungs. "Oh my God, that was terrifying."

The metal rings of the shower curtain clinked as Greg pulled it back and stepped out.

"Dude, you were like Batman," Victor exclaimed, smiling goofily. "You were better than Batman. That was stealth level nine-thousand."

Looking to Wendy, Greg opened his mouth to say something but then paused, sniffing the air.

"Are those pancakes?"

Wendy breathed out a laugh. Picking up one of the to-go boxes, she handed it to him.

"Yep. All yours."

Chapter Fourteen

As soon as the last rays of light had dissipated, Victor was running down some semblance of a plan, marking a starting point on the map and offering alternative places to search for the other Mothmen.

"Vic, they might not be out tonight," Wendy said, watching him make another mark in Sharpie. "It's not like they live in the city."

"Maybe, but they've been seen a bunch already," he said, still writing. "No reason to think we won't spot them. Or that Greg won't, I don't know, sense them."

She glanced over to where Greg was squatted in front of the TV, eating the rest of his hash browns and watching Law and Order with great fascination.

"Maybe," she relented with a sigh. "Okay, I guess we're doing this."

Victor beamed. "We're totally doing this. Greg?"

A short chirp announced he was listening.

"Get your flight gear on, we're wheels up in five."

Greg turned, lifting one dark eyebrow in question. Victor faltered, waving his hands around.

"You know what I mean. We're leaving soon."

Greg nodded and poured the rest of his hash browns into his mouth, using the to-go box as a funnel. Potato bits tumbled out of both corners of his mouth but he didn't seem to notice.

"Wow, is it just me, or did his manners get worse?"

Wendy rolled her eyes. "It's not just you."

As Wendy and Victor put their jackets on, they explained the plan once more.

Greg would follow a general flight path, and Victor would follow in the car as best as he could, while Wendy kept eyes on Greg in the sky. If he found anything important, he'd land and turn on the small flashlight Wendy had given him. If he didn't find anything, they'd regroup in three hours back at the motel.

And with that, Greg was off, climbing up the side of the motel to catch enough wind to soar.

"He could've waited for us to be in the car first," Victor muttered, rushing to get into the driver's seat.

Pittsburg traffic wasn't ideal, but Victor managed to navigate it as gracefully as possible, with only one person honking as he accidentally cut them off.

"Sorry! Sorry," he called, waving and speeding up to get into a turn lane. "Still see him?"

Wendy nodded. "Yep. I think he's actually slowing down for our benefit."

"I don't know if I should be offended or grateful."

"Grateful. If he wanted to leave us in the dust, he could."

Pulling his phone out, Victor used the speech to text option and spoke into the microphone. "Is super fast. Can out-fly a car with no problem."

Snatching his phone from him, Wendy held it up to her face and said, "Wendy officially hates this. Will probably end up getting punched."

Laughing, Victor took his phone back from her and slid it into his jacket pocket. "Hey, this is part of our deal, remember?"

She blinked.

The truth was, she'd forgotten the deal.

Forgotten Victor was helping for any reason other than just being her friend…

"Right. The deal for you to study Greg," she said, turning away from him to stare out her window.

Tense silence filled the car, and Victor started drumming on the steering wheel.

She knew he could sense her mood shift by how often he started looking at her. It was a pattern—stare at the road, check his mirrors, glance at Wendy like a sad puppy, and repeat.

Wendy refused to crack first.

Thankfully, Victor wasn't much for stand-offs.

"I mean, it's not the only reason I'm here," he said. "I know I said you owe me but... Hell, I'd probably still be here even if you'd forced me to be blindfolded and gagged the whole time."

Wendy chuckled. "Really?"

"It'd be mildly uncomfortable, but I'd live," he said, grinning at her. "I'm also not volunteering for that to be our new arrangement."

"Fair enough."

Watching the inky outline of Greg high up in the sky, she thought about Victor's lifelong obsession with all cryptids.

She really couldn't blame him for wanting to keep records. She'd kept a diary about Greg for a few years before she got paranoid someone would find it.

Granted, they probably would have thought she was just writing about an imaginary friend or creating a story for a class assignment.

Maybe someone like Victor would have believed her from the start though...

"Have you always been interested in creatures like Greg?" She asked, tilting her head to glance at Victor.

"Since I was seven or eight, yeah," he said, nodding as he stared out the windshield. "It turned into a full-blown obsession when I was sick."

Straightening, Wendy frowned deeply. "Sick?"

From his expression, she guessed he hadn't meant to drop that detail into the conversation so casually.

"Um, yeah…" Victor turned to check his blind spot as he changed lanes. "I had leukemia as a kid."

The words weighed Wendy's heart down like an anchor, sinking it right into her churning gut.

"I was in the hospital for a while—like, forever," he said, adding a soft laugh. "It was just long days filled with treatments and doctors coming to poke and prod… But my dad brought me books to keep me entertained, and they had all these monsters and myths in them. I couldn't get enough."

Wendy stared at him, influx of emotion threatening to cut off her air supply.

"You… You never told me you'd been sick," she murmured.

Victor shrugged. "It's not really something you can just blurt out, you know? 'Hey, pass the ketchup? Oh, by the way, I had cancer.'" He glanced at her. "It's okay. I've been in remission for years. I get scanned like clockwork and my doctor's the best. If there was something there, he'd find it."

She forced herself to nod. The last thing she wanted was for Victor to mistake her shock for pity.

"Good. I'm really glad you're okay."

In the glow from passing streetlights, Wendy thought she could see color rising up on Victor's cheeks as he smiled softly.

As the silence stretched, the tension turned into ease, thinning the air inside the car.

After a moment, she giggled to herself and Victor looked over.

"What?"

Wendy shook her head. "I'm imagining little Victor Valentine surrounded by huge piles of books written by the driest historians ever, reading about Big Foot and Nessie and… Well," she pointed up, towards the gliding shadow of Greg.

"All while in Incredible Hulk jammies," he said, grinning.

She laughed, covering her mouth. "That's adorable."

"I was a pretty cute kid. Drove my family nuts though." He shifted in his seat, slowing the car down for a red light. "I guess cryptids were like surrogate friends, you know? I couldn't be in school, and the tutoring in the hospital was small and not very intense since we didn't have a lot of energy. I didn't have a lot of people to just… hang out with. But I had them."

It all suddenly clicked.

Wendy had grown up with Greg as a reality. He was her friend, her companion, the only person she trusted more than herself. But she'd known he was real.

Victor had grown up clinging to hope. Fascinated and ravenous for information about creatures that, for all he knew, could be completely fabricated hoaxes. But he chose to believe, and that filled a void when nothing or no one else could.

She'd been wrong.

Greg was just as much a friend to Victor as he was to her. He just hadn't known it.

Wendy wanted to tell him she understood now, that it made sense, that she was sorry for having been a gatekeeper.

Instead, what came out of her mouth was, "I'm sorry I threatened to punch you."

Victor belly laughed. "It's okay. There's no way you hit harder than my sister."

Smiling, Wendy settled back into her seat and turned her attention back to the night sky.

As Victor made a right turn, Greg wasn't visible anymore.

"Wait," she said, reaching for his arm. "I don't see him."

Slowing to a crawl on a mostly empty street, Victor bent to stare up through the windshield. "Did he land?"

"I don't know, I can't—" Just then a small orb of light blinked from the eave of a large church steeple. "There," she said, pointing.

"Moth-kin are hanging out in a church?"

"Really? That's what's surprising for you about this?" She asked, gesturing for him to pull into a free parking spot.

Wendy got out first, staring up at the church, searching for Greg in the night.

"Hey, do you hear that?" Victor asked, coming up behind her. "It sounds like…"

"Chirping," she finished for him. "Greg's talking."

"I don't think it's just Greg."

Grabbing Victor by the sleeve, Wendy started jogging towards the church. "C'mon."

* * * * * * *

December 1st, 2007

"What would happen if other people met you?"

Greg looked down from the branch he'd landed on, waiting for Wendy to catch up in her climb.

His head tilted to the side in thought.

"I'm not sure," he clicked. *"I've tried before. Most people are afraid of me."*

Wendy grunted as she swung her leg up, using it to pull herself onto a higher branch.

"I'm not," she said, puffing her cheeks out.

Greg wheezed a laugh. **"You were at first."**

"Nuh-uh! You just startled me, is all."

"Suuuuure."

Squinting at him, she stuck her tongue out and made a rude noise, which only got Greg to laugh harder.

"Doesn't it make you sad?" Wendy leaned back against the tree trunk, staring up at his black velveteen silhouette. *"That no one else wants to get to know you?"*

Shaking out his wings, Greg hummed a noise like he was copying the sounds Wendy made when she was thinking.

"Sometimes. I don't have a lot of friends."

"You have me," she announced proudly, plucking at the straps of her denim overalls.

He nodded, grinning. **"I know I have you. But you get to have lots of other friends too."**

Wendy considered that for a moment.

The other kids in her class were nice, and she saw Rebecca the most, playing with her after school when Darlene was working late. She still didn't feel like she was that close with any of them. And she definitely couldn't trust any of them with knowing about Greg.

Reaching inside the chest flap of her overalls, she pulled out the braided embroidery thread bracelet she'd made during recess. She'd planned to give it to her mom, but she was feeling a change of heart.

"Hey, Greg," she called, looking up at him. "I have something for you."

When he turned on his branch to face her, she held it out for him.

"What is it?"

"It's a bracelet," she said. "I made it for you."

Two long talons gently grasped the school supply creation. **"For me? What does it mean?"**

"It's a friendship bracelet. I have one too, see?" Wendy held up her left wrist, showing off her knotted blue and yellow accessory. "It means we're best friends."

Greg blinked his reddish-brown eyes, staring down at the gift cradled in his palm.

"Thank you, Wendy," he chirped softly. After a moment of struggle, he managed to slip it on and tighten the ends to secure it. **"I love it."**

"I thought you might." Wendy smiled, and turned her attention to the setting winter sun.

It was decided.

Greg and Wendy were best friends forever.

* * * * * * *

Victor yanked on the door to the church to no avail.

"So much for sanctuary," he muttered, staring up at the stained-glass windows. "Can you make out what they're saying?"

Wendy backed up, trying to see the other Mothman Greg was talking to.

"Sort of… Something about a building." She frowned, watching the beam of light sway and flicker. "Greg's explaining what a flashlight is."

"Guess not every Mothman has a Wendy."

The clicking came to an abrupt halt and Wendy grabbed Victor by the back of his jacket.

"They heard you," she whispered. "The other one is getting spooked."

She could understand Greg's urgent explanation beneath the scrapes and flapping of wings.

"It's okay, she's my friend. And he's… harmless."

"They're not afraid?"

"No, not at all. Wendy is special and kind. She's my best friend."

Warmth spread through her chest as she listened.

Before she could translate for Victor, a sharp siren made them both jump and spin around. Flashing blue lights blinded them as a police car pulled up to the curb only a few feet away.

"Oh no…" Victor stepped closer, holding onto Wendy's arm.

"Is there a problem?" One of the officers asked, holding a flashlight up to shine in their faces.

"Uh, no sir," Wendy called. "We were… We just…"

"You have business in that church?"

Panic bubbled in her chest. Words wouldn't come to her as she stared at the approaching patrolmen.

"We were just leaving," Victor said, trying to pull Wendy towards the car.

Just as one of them was about to stop him, a terrifying screech echoed from above. The officer nearly dropped his flashlight as he jerked.

A huge creature swooped down from the roof, the tip of its wing knocking the policeman off his feet as it dive-bombed.

"Holy shit!" The officer yelled, covering his head with one arm as he reached for his gun.

"No!" Wendy cried, starting to bolt for him. But she couldn't move—something had her.

Victor had grabbed her around the waist, holding her back with a strength she hadn't known he possessed.

"Wendy, don't," he pleaded as she struggled against him. "Don't."

Then a second creature flew at them, and the officer shouted in fear, leaving his gun in his holster as he rolled away from the thing attacking him.

"We have to go. We have to go *now*," Victor told her, hauling Wendy towards the car.

The second officer was braced behind his passenger door, aiming for the two Mothmen circling them.

Wendy froze, gasping in horror as she stared.

A shot rang out, and Victor covered her head as they both ducked beside their Subaru.

"Greg!" She screamed.

"Wendy, c'mon, c'mon," he urged, opening her door and shoving her inside.

It was chaos.

Flapping wings and furious shrieking. Several more gunshots.

Victor peeled away, going sixty down a residential street.

Wendy turned, gripping the back of the headrest as she stared out the back windshield. "We can't leave him!" She shouted.

Making a sharp left, Victor didn't take his eyes off the road. "We have to. There's nothing we can do now."

"Those cops—"

"Were shooting at them, and they would have shot at us if we tried to stop them."

"Victor--!"

"*No!*"

It was the first time she'd ever heard him yell that loudly.

"I'm not letting something happen to you just 'cause you're trying to protect Greg! I'm not." He shook his head, jaw so tense the muscle ticked.

Helpless, and unable to form an argument, Wendy slumped against the back of her seat and watched the city blur behind their car.

Chapter Fifteen

Victor parked in the motel lot and turned the ignition off.

Wringing his hands over the wheel a few times, he took a deep breath.

"Look, I know… You have every right to be mad at me." He sighed. "But I just—I couldn't put you in danger like that."

Wendy didn't say a word.

"And, I mean, this isn't Greg's first brush with freaked out people holding guns. He's fast, he's agile, he's—"

Wendy clutched Victor's forearm suddenly.

"He's on the roof," she gasped, scrambling to get out of the car.

"Oh—Oh my god!"

She bolted across the lot, ignoring Victor's sounds of distress as he got tangled in his seatbelt and choked himself.

"Greg? Are you okay?"

The dark shadow glided down and landed in a crouch a few feet from her.

"Of course," Greg chirped. *"That's not the first time I've been shot at."*

Dropping down, she crushed herself to him in a bear hug.

"You scared me half to death."

"Sorry."

"Dude," Victor called, tripping as he ran over. "What happened? Where's the other one?"

Before Greg could answer, Wendy was ordering them inside the motel room to avoid prying eyes.

"She didn't follow me," Greg clicked, lumbering over to the foot of one of the beds. *"I told her it was safe here, but…"*

Wendy translated as she yanked her jacket off and tossed it over the chair by the TV.

"Did she say where she and the other Moth-folk are living?" Victor asked.

"No. I'd barely introduced myself when everything happened."

"Well that's a little frustrating," Victor muttered after Wendy relayed. "But she told you why they were making themselves known, right?"

Greg shrugged. *"Sort of?"*

Flapping his arms out in annoyance, Victor gaped. "What does that even *mean*?"

"Cut it out, Vic," Wendy said, resting her hand on Greg's shoulder. "We've already had a rough enough night."

Sighing, Victor ran a hand over his face. "You're right. I'm just…" He held Greg's stare for a beat. "I'm glad you're okay, man. You scared us."

With an expression like a pleased cat, Greg nodded and chirped, *"I think he likes me."*

Wendy smiled. "You're not wrong."

Pulling his jacket off and chucking it onto the bed, Victor massaged his neck. "I'm taking a shower," he said, wandering over to his bag to retrieve toiletries and sleep clothes. "I smell like stress sweat and drive-thru."

"You're telling me," Greg clicked under his breath, and Wendy elbowed him. *"Ow."*

"Be nice," she hissed.

Victor stopped in the bathroom doorway, turning around. "I know you're talking about me, but I'm going to let it slide this time." He pointed at them both. "*This* time."

When she heard the shower cut on, Wendy arranged herself on the edge of the bed by Greg. "What aren't you telling me?"

"Huh? Nothing."

"Liar. I can always tell 'cause your little ear tips wiggle."

Greg reached up to tug on his right ear, furrowing his brows. *"It's involuntary."*

"Greg…"

Sighing—which sounded more like a donkey groaning—he sat back on his heels and looked up at her. *"She said... She remembered me."*

Wendy straightened instantly. "She knew you? Knew you from before?"

Greg chirped an affirmative and nodded. *"But that was all before we heard the police siren."*

"What about the building?" She asked, frowning. "I heard you two talking about it when we walked up."

"She said they can hear the vibrations inside a building," he explained. *"Like what I heard with the bridge. They just can't figure out where yet."*

"So that's why they kept climbing up the Fort Pitt," Wendy said. "They were trying to hear better."

Greg nodded. *"Being too close to the street makes it hard to listen to anything. The sounds bounce off concrete. It's... confusing."*

Wendy's eyes widened in fascination.

A Mothman brand of echolocation.

"Did she say anything else?"

Greg frowned, glancing at his hands. *"No. But..."*

"What is it?"

"You were right," he clicked. *"I'm not alone. I'm not the only one."*

She smiled, reaching for one of his talons. "I told you, Greg. You have family." She swallowed. "Well, *more* family."

"So... What do I do?"

"I think first we have to find them again," she said. "But it looks like maybe you have a decision to make."

Grunting softly, he lifted a brow as if to say 'I guess' and rolled his shoulders.

Moments after the shower cut off, the door swung open and Victor came out in a soft, worn out Ohio State tee and sweatpants, toweling his hair dry.

"Okay, so I know we're all exhausted, but hear me out—Oreos and making fun of the worst movie we can find on cable. Any takers?"

Greg looked to Wendy, a grin curling his thin lips.

"I think Greg's interested at least," she said with a laugh.

"Great, I'm going to raid the vending machine," Victor said, tossing his towel back into the bathroom.

As he maneuvered around them towards the door, Greg watched Victor over his shoulder before turning back to Wendy, eyebrows raised in a knowing way she'd never seen before.

"What?" She asked.

"Nothing," Greg chirped, unconvincingly.

Wendy scowled, listening to Victor leave.

It took her several seconds before she put the pieces together.

"Oh my God, you're not... You don't think..." She laughed a little too sharply. "Oh please."

"You're turning red."

Wendy waved him off. "Because I'm suffering from second-hand embarrassment. For *you*. 'Cause you're so unbelievably wrong."

Greg smirked—an odd little quirk of his mouth—and simply stared at her.

"Shut up," she said, pushing him off balance with her foot. "You're the worst."

"Nuh-uh," he chirped, teasing her.

Pointing a finger at him, she said, "I'm not going to let Victor give you any Oreos if you keep it up."

"I'm sure he'd rather give them all to you, anyway."

Wendy shoved him with a shocked laugh, and Greg flapped his wings to keep his balance, almost knocking over a lamp.

"Rude," he clicked, snickering.

Crossing her legs, Wendy chewed her thumbnail for a moment before groaning. "He is kind of cute, huh?"

"Who's cute?" Victor asked as he reentered the room, arms full of junk food.

Greg let out a croaking wheeze of a laugh and Wendy pushed him back with a palm to the face.

"You," he chirped, muffled by her fingers.

Wendy blinked. "Uh, Michael... Cera," she covered awkwardly.

Staring at her like she'd just spoken Latin, Victor dumped their vending machine feast on his bed. "Didn't realize you had a thing for the guy from *Juno*... But I'm not judging."

Greg simply laughed again as Wendy glared daggers at him.

And she definitely stole most of his Oreos.

* * * * * * *

Wendy woke up in a mostly dark room, the television still flickering with a muted Lifetime Channel movie.

Rolling over, she squinted, trying to orient herself.

Greg lay stretched out between the two beds, like an overgrown pet, with his wings wrapped around his shoulders. Soft snoring never faltered, so she knew he'd been asleep for a while.

The opposite bed was empty though—didn't even look slept in—and all evidence of junk food had been cleaned off.

"Vic?" She whispered.

"Hey, I'm over here," he said, turning around in his seat at the desk-slash-TV stand.

Sitting up, Wendy attempted to push her hair back but got caught in a tangle of curls. "What time is it?"

"Late. Er, well, early I guess is more accurate."

Extricating herself from the stiff motel comforter, she tip-toed around Greg to see what Victor was prioritizing above sleep.

The city map was spread over the table, and he was scribbling notes on a few sheets of paper that seemed to correspond to numbers marked on certain streets and landmarks.

"This seems… Complicated," she said, rubbing the corner of her eye.

"I couldn't sleep," he admitted, glancing up. "I kept thinking about what you and Greg told me—about the vibrations and the building and noise confusion."

Still groggy, Wendy tried to follow. "Okay, and did you come up with an idea?"

"About a dozen," he said, tapping his pen on the map. "I started listing similarities between what the lady Moth-kin said and what happened with the Silver Bridge collapse. Lots of traffic or use, large structures, metal cable—"

Wendy frowned, shaking her head. "Vic?"

He stared up at her. "I think the Mothmen can hear something wrong because it's coming from a taller building. And I think it has to be a building with lots of steel cable being used, which would probably mean elevators. A lot of them."

Squatting next to the desk, she folded her arms along the edge of the tabletop and examined the map closely.

Victor had marked the locations of the tallest buildings in Pittsburg.

"You think the Mothmen can hear an elevator cable about to snap?"

"Or multiples. If the quality of the wires isn't great, they could all go at the same time. My dad's a lawyer, he's sued a ton of shoddy construction companies for using faulty materials to cut costs." Victor looked to his notes again. "If it's happening in a taller building, the damage could be—"

"Catastrophic," Wendy finished for him, cold dread skipping down her spine. "Vic, what do we do?"

"Uh, my vote was to impersonate a building inspector and tell everyone to get their elevators serviced."

"Victor."

He flailed his arms a bit dramatically and said, "Well, I don't know. How are we supposed to get them to listen to us? We're college kids, we're only seen as real adults when it comes to drinking and student loan debt."

Inhaling deeply, Wendy thought for a moment. "Maybe we can try to narrow down which building it is? Then we could call in an anonymous tip."

"That's a very specific anonymous tip."

Wendy bit the inside of her cheek. "And it's going to take us all day to find out which high-rise the sound is coming from."

"How are we supposed to keep Greg hidden in broad daylight?" Victor asked, turning to look at him as he snored through their conversation.

"I don't think we can."

Grimacing, Victor dropped his pen on top of the map. "I officially hate my own plan."

Reaching over, she gently rubbed his arm from shoulder to elbow crease and back.

"It'll be okay," Wendy said. "We'll figure it out."

A warm hand covered hers and she glanced up.

"Hey, about today..." He started. "At the church..."

Wendy smiled softly. "We're good, Vic. I promise."

Big brown eyes stared at her for a moment before he nodded.

Standing up, she went back to her bed, tiptoeing around Greg once more and crawling under the comforter.

As she settled back in, she gazed at the ceiling as a knot twisted in her stomach.

Wendy longed for the day when the plan had been simple—Find the other Mothmen, introduce Greg, see if they wanted to be friends.

That day felt like a hazy dream from years ago. Something barely remembered or tangible.

Wendy drifted back to sleep wishing for simplicity.

Chapter Sixteen

"Dude, hold still."

Greg's clicking could be heard through the bathroom door as Wendy patted her curls dry.

"I'm trying. You're the jittery one."

"Okay, I don't know what you just said, but there was *tone*, so I'm taking offense."

Opening the door, Wendy frowned. "What are you doing?"

Halting with the end of a measuring tape in his mouth, Victor turned.

"Takin' measurements," he said between clenched teeth.

She tilted her head to look at Greg as he held the other end of the tape. "Is that so…"

"It's for his notes," Greg clicked. *"He wanted more accuracy."*

Wendy smirked. "Well, don't let me stop you," she said, hanging her towel up.

Jotting down Greg's arm span, Victor then pointed to his wings. "Mind opening those up? Let's see what we're working with here."

Making sure he wouldn't knock anything over, Greg angled himself and spread his wings in a dramatic flair that startled Victor into taking a step back.

"Whoa," he said, jaw slackening. "I mean, I saw them folded, and while you were flying but not this close…" He leaned in, poking at the thinner membranes of skin stretched across bone. "They're like bat wings but… Kind of softer. And darker. I can't see the blood vessels through these like with other flying mammals." He looked up at Greg. "Are you technically a mammal?"

Lifting one distinct eyebrow, Greg shrugged.

"I think he is," Wendy commented, pulling her shoes on. "He has some bird and reptile qualities, but he has a more mammalian metabolism and he doesn't go dormant when it's cold, so…"

Victor tipped his head back to look Greg in the eyes. "You're like a cryptid platypus."

Greg's wet wheeze of a laugh made Victor beam.

"Okay, just a few more measurements and we're good."

Wendy watched from the foot of her bed, a smile curving her lips.

Victor was having the time of his life, child-like enthusiasm pouring out of him as he rushed around with his notebook, pen, and easily tangled measuring tape. All the anthropology classes he'd taken were showing in his double and triple checking of collected data.

At least Greg didn't seem to mind the inspection.

Feeling someone staring at her, she blinked and looked up to see Greg grinning like a cat who ate a whole canary family.

'You're not funny,' she mouthed at him, glaring.

"Yes, I am."

Victor paused his note taking. "Huh?"

"Nothing," Wendy said hurriedly. "Greg's just hungry."

"Well, that is true, but…"

"I just need two more minutes, big guy, and then we can hit up a drive-thru."

As Victor turned, Wendy caught a glimpse of the tee shirt under his plaid button down, and sputtered.

"Victor, what the hell are you wearing?"

Tucking his pen behind his ear, he ducked behind Greg's wing. "Uh, well… Remember in Point Pleasant when you ran to get coffee and I said I went to gas up the car? I did. But I also stopped into a store and…"

"And bought an 'I believe in Mothman' shirt?" She gestured to his outfit.

Jotting down another measurement, Victor popped his head out from behind Greg. "It's my color," he said sheepishly. "Plus, I do believe." Patting Greg on the arm, he looked up. "I believe in you, man."

Greg nodded once. *"Thank you, I appreciate that."*

"You might look good in red, but it isn't exactly subtle given who our traveling companion is," Wendy argued, waving a hand out at Greg.

As Greg began to click at her teasingly, Victor tugged at his clothes.

"Well do you want me to change?"

Wendy took a deep breath.

It wasn't the end of the world if he wore the shirt, and he did like it a lot…

"No," she sighed. "It's fine. Just hurry up, please? I'm starving."

Victor's celebratory fist pump almost made her smile.

Almost. She hadn't had enough coffee to be cheery yet.

True to his word, Victor finished taking his measurements and then bought Greg as many egg and cheese bagels as he could stomach.

"Is it safe for him to eat all that before flying?" Victor asked, watching Greg in the rearview scarf down his food, a bagel in each hand. "He's going to get a cramp or something."

Wendy just laughed. "Remind me to tell you about the time I bought a bunch of discounted sheet cake from the Wal-Mart just outside town and bet Greg he couldn't eat it all, do forty barrel-rolls, and not puke."

Victor paused with his paper coffee cup to his lips. "That sounds... Like it has a disgusting ending."

"Oh, it does. But probably not how you're imagining."

"Consider me hooked," Victor said. At a red light, he twisted around. "You're sure you're okay with this, Greg?"

"They could use some barbeque sauce, but otherwise they're pretty good."

Wendy snorted a laugh. "He meant with doing fly-by's of all these buildings."

"Oh." Greg blinked at them. *"Of course I am."*

"He's fine," she said. "Which one is first?"

Pulling his phone from his pocket, Victor opened his note app and handed his cell to her. "I listed them all by distance from the motel to make this a little more efficient."

Nodding, Wendy read the names and then glanced back. "'Kay Greg, you fueled up enough?"

Patting his full belly, he nodded. *"Point the way."*

Finding a deserted alley to idle in, Greg got out of the car and stayed low, awkwardly hopping away and out of public view. They waited for him to scale the side of the apartment building and disappear onto the roof before pulling back onto the street.

"Nervous?" Victor asked.

"No." She wrinkled her nose. "Okay, yes. Very."

"I have anxiety Twizzlers in the glove box if you need something to chew on that isn't your thumbnail."

She opened her mouth to retort and then stopped, mood shifting. "I love Twizzlers."

"You're welcome."

* * * * * * *

After the third near miss with another car, Wendy insisted on driving.

Forcing Victor to pull over, she chastised him for not getting enough sleep.

"Caffeine isn't a substitute for rest, you know," she said, closing the driver's side door.

"Oh, that's rich, coming from the girl who lives on the stuff."

She fumbled with the seat adjustment and rolled her eyes. "That's different. I'm trying to graduate early to save money, and the only way to do that is by doubling up my class load."

"Excuses, excuses…"

Wendy glared at him. "Would you just buckle up already? We're going to lose Greg."

"No, we're not, he's right…" Victor started to point and then dropped his hand. "Oh."

"Yeah. *Oh.*"

Victor clicked his seatbelt and gestured in front of him. "Well, he couldn't have gotten far."

"Says the guy who literally has a note in his phone that says, 'super fast, can out-fly a car,'" she muttered, pulling into traffic and changing lanes.

"You know what, Wendy—" Victor cut himself off, staring forward with a clenched jaw.

Inhaling, he scrubbed his palm over his face and started to laugh.

"I knew you didn't get enough sleep," she said. "You're totally loopy."

Victor shook his head. "I don't know what it says about us that we're bickering like an old married couple, but it's pretty damn funny."

Adjusting the mirror, Wendy smirked. "My parents never fought like that."

"No?"

"Nope," she said. "Probably why they got divorced."

Victor laughed. "Yikes." Taking a moment to sober himself, he added, "I didn't mean to snap."

"It's alright, you're tired."

"Still, it was uncalled for."

Looking over, she struggled against the urge to tease him. "You're too hard on yourself, Vic. You didn't even hurt my feelings."

He smiled softly. "Now I know you're not mad."

"Huh?"

"You only call me 'Vic' if you're not upset. Any other time it's 'Victor' like you're going to strangle me with the consonants in my own name."

Wendy's cheeks flushed. She hadn't realized he'd noticed her name choices for him at all, let alone picked up on the emotional correlations.

She was so glad Greg wasn't in the car.

"Don't worry, I don't mind," he said, still smiling.

"Well, as long as it isn't annoying…" She said, focusing intently on the street ahead. "Do you see him?"

Victor shook his head. "No, not yet. But keep going this way, One PPG Place is only a few blocks away."

"How many more are on the list?"

"Um… A lot. But maybe we'll find the right place soon."

Wendy kept her doubts to herself.

"Hey, is that…" Victor leaned forward, staring up at the sky. "Either that's Greg, or we've got another Moth-kin joining us."

Taking the next turn so slowly the car behind her honked, Wendy searched for Greg between the high-rise buildings.

"That... Might not be Greg," she said, spotting the winged creature in the distance.

It looked smaller than Greg, with a shorter wingspan, and lighter coloring.

"Lady Moth then?"

Wendy squinted. She hadn't gotten a good look the night before, but it was possible.

"Do you think they're looking for the building?" She asked. "Or for Greg?"

"I don't know. Do Moth-folk sense each other in flight? I wonder if they have flocking tendencies, like geese when they migrate." Victor made a frustrated noise at the back of his throat. "See, this is *exactly* why we need a crypto-anthropology class at school."

"I don't think now is the best time to get on your soap box, Vic," she said, ignoring the catch in her voice when she used his nickname.

"Fine, fine... But I'm still going to try to convince Doctor Bledsoe."

Wendy tapped the edge of his phone, pointing at the list of buildings. "First thing's first."

"Speaking of, take a left. Moth-kin are bearing off course."

* * * * * * *

Wendy dropped her last quarters into the meter as Victor locked up the car.

"I don't know," he said, stepping up onto the curb. "You really think searching on foot is a good idea?"

"We've been driving around for forty-five minutes and we haven't spotted either of them." Wendy started off towards the next high-rise on Victor's list. "At least this way we might hear them talking if they're close."

A fire truck sped up the street, siren blaring as it took a sharp corner.

Victor winced and rubbed his left ear. "Oh yeah, we'll definitely be able to hear them."

Rolling her eyes, Wendy grabbed his jacket sleeve and yanked. "C'mon."

Weaving around small clusters of pedestrians, they followed the GPS on Victor's phone to the next building, eyes glued to the skyline. No dark winged figures, no rapid clicks.

Dread filled Wendy's chest, slowing her breathing and pinching her ribs together.

What if they'd lost him? What if something happened? What if—

"This way," Victor said, interrupting her spiral as he guided her across the street. "It's a block away."

"Something doesn't feel right, Vic," she said, arching her neck to stare at the rooftops around them.

"We're almost there."

As they hurried, Wendy squinted into the distance, noting yellow caution tape flapping in X formations along a large scaffolding structure.

"Oh no…" She murmured, taking off at a jog.

Before they could get too close to the building, a large man in a yellow hardhat stepped in front of them, a meaty hand raised at chest level.

"Whoa, hey, where'd you think you're going?"

Victor skidded to a halt, mere centimeters from Wendy. "Uh… We were…"

"This is a construction zone," the man said, jerking his thumb over his shoulder. "You're going to have to go around."

"Construction?" Victor asked as the man was already turning away.

"That's what I said."

Wendy shifted closer. "Um, sorry, but what kind of construction?"

The foreman eyed her, annoyed as well as confused why anyone would care to ask.

"Elevators were breaking down," he said, glancing down at the clipboard in his hand. "Got in there and found out the whole cable system was bad. Have to replace everything, just like the others."

"Others?"

He sighed through his nose. "Yeah, the other buildings that used the same construction company. What, are you going to be tested on this later?"

Victor made a move to intervene, but Wendy continued.

"Oh, sorry," she said, flashing a smile and tucking a curl behind her ear. "My uncle works at a real estate firm down the street. I didn't know if I should be telling him to warn his bosses their elevators are about to turn into death traps."

The considerable crevasse between the foreman's brows lessened and he shook his head. "Nah, this company only did a few gigs before folding. We're playing catch up though."

Victor caught her by the wrist, tugging gently. "Okay, thank you," he said, guiding them back to the cross walk as he stared at his phone.

"What are you doing?" Wendy whispered. "I was about to ask him which other buildings were affected."

"I know, and you don't have to," he said. "I saw the defunct company name on his clipboard and Googled it. Look." Victor showed her his phone, with an article pulled up about the ongoing civil case. "Most of the buildings are four or five stories but there are two high rises. That one—" He gestured over his shoulder. "And the BNY Mellon Center."

Wendy's face fell. "That's eight blocks away."

"Yep, so we should hurry," he said, starting to run with her in tow.

Dodging traffic and pedestrians crowding the sidewalks, they bolted towards the skyscraper.

"Vic, do you hear that?" Wendy asked.

He stared at her like she'd grown another head.

"You're kidding right? All I hear is my heart exploding," he panted.

Grabbing him by the jacket, she forced him to slow down. "Listen," she said. "I think I hear screeching."

"As in Moth-kin screeching?"

Wendy nodded. "Something's wrong," she said, taking off again at a sprint.

"Wen—Wait," Victor called, running after her.

They could see the plaza and a crowd of people gathering in front of the building, staring up with their hands shielding their eyes from the sun.

"Vic…" Wendy breathed, hand going to her throat. "Look."

Circling the roof of the Mellon Center, were two large winged creatures, shrieking and crying out at the people below.

Victor stopped dead. "What are they doing?"

"I don't know," she said, shaking her head. "Are they trying to warn people?"

One of them swooped down, knocking against the windows along the top floors before pushing away from the side and flying upwards once more.

Gaze darting from the building's entrance to the Mothmen above, Victor frowned. "I… I think they're trying to get people out."

Horrified, Wendy reached for him. "Does that mean something's about to happen?"

"I don't know, I don't know," he said hurriedly, running his hand through his hair.

"We have to do something, Vic!"

"What *can* we do?" He asked, panic hitching his voice. "How do we get people to believe us?"

More people gathered nearby, watching in astonishment as the two creatures circled and dove through the air, smacking the sides of the Mellon Center with terrifying strength. Soon nearly everyone had their phones out, videoing the bizarre spectacle.

One woman nearby glanced over, and in a second, she did a double take, whipping her head around to squint at Victor's shirt.

Staring down at himself, Victor yelped, and grabbed the sides of his jacket, quickly covering his torso and folding his arms tightly across his chest.

"You were right, this was not a subtle shirt to wear while hunting Moth-kin," he said, leaning closer to Wendy.

"Victor, I need you to listen," she said, turning to him. "You have to go inside and find a way to pull the fire alarm. That will keep people out of the elevators."

His frown deepened but he nodded. "Okay, and then what?"

"I'm not sure yet, but we have to keep people outside until we can warn someone about the steel cables."

"Wendy—"

"Go, Vic," she said, pushing him towards the building.

As he turned away, Wendy stared up at Greg's shadowy form backlit in the sky.

"Please... please don't be mad," she whispered.

Taking a deep breath, Wendy closed her eyes.

"Oh my God, that's Mothman!"

Chapter Seventeen

September 21st, 2012

Pushing the stubborn shopping cart with as much effort as she could, Wendy followed her dad up and down the aisles of Harry's Hardware.

She always managed to get the cart with the broken wheel. Like she had cart karma from a previous life.

"C'mon, sport," John said over his shoulder. "Can't spend all day here."

Wendy blew out a heavy breath. "I'm trying daddy," she muttered, shoving the buggy and nearly careening it into a display of eco-friendly cleaning supplies.

The bell above the door chimed just before she heard a man holler.

"I saw him! I swear to God, I—It was him! I know it was!"

Everyone in the store halted, turning to get a look at whoever was causing a ruckus.

Peering around the corner, John and Wendy frowned.

"Isn't that Jim from church?" She asked in a whisper.

"Sure is," John said. "He looks like he's seen a ghost..."

As the owner of the store attempted to comfort the man, John wandered closer.

"Hey there, Jim," he said. "You alright?"

Wide eyed, Jim turned to face him. "I saw him. Out in the woods behind the old manufacturing plant. I just..." *Wrenching his ball cap off his head, he scrubbed the sweat from his brow before glancing behind him.* "Harry, you got anymore shotgun shells?"

"Jim, why don't you tell me what's got you so rattled," *John said, tucking his hands into his pockets.*

"I saw him. I saw that devil Mothman."

Wendy gasped sharply, covering her mouth with both hands.

"Well, now, hold on..." *John started.*

"That thing is pure evil, John," *he said, voice rising.* "You didn't see it, you didn't look in its eyes. I'm telling you, it's one of Satan's creatures."

"No, he's not," *Wendy yelled, abandoning the cursed shopping cart as she rushed forward.* "He is not evil!"

John stared at her, bewildered. "Honey, it's okay, Jim's just a little nervous is all—"

"Nervous? I'll show you nervous," *Jim said, handing cash over to Harry as he picked up the box of shells.* "I'll make that flying demon wish he'd never been born."

Wendy's vision tunneled. He was threatening Greg...

Snarling through gritted teeth, she ran passed her father and with two hands, shoved Jim with such force he nearly tumbled into the patio grilling mock up.

"What the—"

"You leave him alone," *she screamed, tearing the box from his hands and hurling it to the floor.* "He's never hurt anyone! You leave him be!"

Tripping and skidding on strewn shotgun shells, John tried his best to pull Wendy off an utterly dazed Jim.

"Wendy! Wendy, stop!"

She'd never understood what people meant when they said they 'saw red' until that day.

That day Wendy went blind with the color.

"The only devil here is you," *she shouted, kicking Jim's shin as she continued to push him.* "How dare you try to hurt G—"

"Wendy!" *John bellowed, finally hooking an arm around her waist and yanking her back.* "Stop it, right now!"

With a little distance, she could see the havoc she'd brought down on the entryway to Harry's Hardware. And in the middle, a red-faced Jim with his hat knocked off, barely able to regain his balance.

"Calm down, Wendy, calm down," *her father said in her ear as he continued to walk her backwards.*

Pulling himself together, Jim glared at both of them. "You better put a leash on her," he snapped, before stooping down to grab his cap and storm out, leaving his shotgun shells all over the linoleum floor.

Catching her breath, Wendy's cheeks burned as she became fully aware of all the people staring at her.

"Come on," John urged, taking her by the arm. "Let's go."

Blind fury dissolved into embarrassed tears she refused to cry as Wendy followed her dad out to the parking lot.

She didn't say a word as she opened the door and got in. Instead, she stared at the scuffed toes of her Converse sneakers and the frayed heel of her jeans her mother had insisted were too long for her.

Sliding his key into the ignition, John sighed and leaned back in his seat without starting the engine.

Each moment felt like an eternity. Wendy was certain she'd be trapped in that car forever, forced to count the grooves in the floor mats as penance.

A broken sound escaped her dad, but she was too afraid to look up.

Then another, a little gravellier, and another…

Curiosity got the better of her.

Wendy glanced over, expecting the worst.

John's lips were pinched together in a tight line as his whole body shook. The wrinkles at the corners of his eyes deepened as his head tilted from side to side.

Before Wendy could open her mouth to speak, her dad lost whatever battle he'd been fighting with himself.

Raucous laughter exploded from his chest, echoing around the car's interior and ringing in Wendy's ears.

John doubled over, gripping the steering wheel for support as he guffawed.

He'd lost it. She'd made her dad lose his marbles.

"Daddy?"

"Did you see Jim's face?" He wheezed. "Like you were a banshee coming for his soul. My God, I've never seen a grown man so terrified in my life."

Wendy blinked.

"You started wailin' on him and I thought he was going to piss himself," John continued to laugh. "Even Harry looked spooked."

Renewed heat flooded her face and she sunk further down in her seat. "I... I didn't mean to..."

*"What **was** that Wendy?" He asked, leaning one elbow on the steering wheel. "You've never done anything like that."*

Staring down at her lap, she shook her head. "I don't know... I just..." She inhaled deeply. "I didn't want Jim to hurt him."

Sobering, John wiped the corners of his eyes. "Hurt who?" He paused a moment before adding, "Mothman?"

Wendy decided to let her silence be her answer.

"Goodness, darlin', that's what got you riled up? Jim threatenin' to go after Mothman?" He sighed, releasing some tension from his shoulders. "Honey, you know very well I'm not a skeptic—I mean, I've seen my fair share of strange occurrences—but even if Jim did see Mothman, do you really think he'd manage to find him again? And then get a clear shot at him?"

Fidgeting with the nylon strap across her hips, Wendy shrugged. "I guess not."

"Besides, Jim's not a very good aim anyway. He'd probably waste all his shot in the trees before he even clipped Mothman."

Wendy tried to feel comforted, but the danger had been so real, so tangible, it still churned in her gut.

"I didn't realize you were so concerned about our little town legend," he added softly.

She wanted to correct him.

Greg was anything but little.

"I just… don't think it's fair for people to assume something's evil when he can't even defend himself."

John turned in his seat, watching her. "Wendy, do you believe in Mothman? Have you seen him?"

It was her chance. A wide open doorway to step through and share the burden of truth she'd been carrying for years.

Her dad would believe her. He'd had he's own experiences, even before her friendship with Greg had come along. If anyone in her family would understand, it would be him.

And how amazed would he be if he got to **meet** Greg?

Fear flooded her system, making her legs wobble.

It was too risky. The more people who knew, the more dangerous it would be for Greg. She wouldn't be able to protect him or keep him hidden.

What they had wouldn't be as special anymore…

Wendy glanced up, holding her father's gaze.

"No, daddy," she said. "I've never seen him."

A hint of disappointment darkened his eyes, but he nodded. "I guess that's just as well," he said. "Not everybody can get that chance, I suppose."

Turning, John opened his door and started to get out.

"Where are you going?" She asked.

"Going to help Harry sweep up those shells you tossed," he said, leaning down to look at her. "And then I guess I better buy Jim an apology gift. Maybe he'll take a new tackle box."

Just before he closed the door, Wendy said, "I'm really sorry, dad."

Smiling, John shook his head. "We all have our moments. Just… try not to assault anyone else, okay? Harry's only got so many fishing supplies."

Wendy laughed quietly and watched him go back inside the hardware store.

As the afternoon sun waned, she made a decision.

No one else, for as long as she lived, would know she believed in Mothman.

* * * * * * *

Powering through her embarrassment, Wendy raised her voice once more.

"That's Mothman!"

The people closest to her turned, staring in confusion. But they didn't move away.

Part of them wanted to believe too.

"It's Mothman! Look!" She shouted, pointing at the sky.

Across the street, she saw Victor halt at the glass doors and turn back, bewilderment evident even from a distance.

Gesturing subtly, she urged him to keep going. Victor's arms flailed in protest, or misunderstanding. Or both. Wendy urged him onward, refusing to get into a miming argument in the middle of the street.

Finally, after what felt like a lifetime, he relented and wove through a stream of people exiting the building to get inside.

A murmur rippled through the crowd, growing louder and surer with every repeat.

Mothman was there. Mothman was in Pittsburg.

And he had a friend.

The pit in Wendy's stomach doubled in size every time she heard another person say the name.

Her plan was working though. More and more people exited the Mellon Center, phones in hand to capture grainy video and photos of the unknown.

Every ounce of her wanted to tell them to stop. To leave him alone.

She wanted to go back to being a child in the McClintic Wildlife Preserve, skipping rocks and building forts with the best friend she couldn't tell anyone she had.

Her wrist itched with the absence of the friendship bracelet she'd worn every day until it unraveled Junior year of high school.

The Mothmen continued to fly above, hitting the windows in succession as they screeched.

A shrill alarm sounded from inside as lights flashed. Everyone in the crowd turned as more and more people fled the building.

"Oh God," one woman said, angling her phone. "They're setting off the alarm or something."

Wendy bit the inside of her cheek. Now wasn't the time to correct someone on legitimate Mothman abilities.

Concern and fear mingled in everyone's voices as they turned to each other, asking what was happening and why. More people crowded the sidewalks, pushing Wendy along like a current she didn't want to stay in.

A familiar head of tousled brown hair could be seen through the thick wall of people across the street. "Wendy?"

"Over here," she called back to Victor, extricating herself from the others.

As he split away from the herd, he darted across the street for her. "I think someone spotted me, so we got to go," he said quietly.

"But we have to figure out how to tell them—"

"Wendy, we can't," he interrupted. "This is more attention than even I'm comfortable with, so we got to make like a banana peel and—"

Seeing a newspaper box, Wendy climbed on top and pulled her phone out.

"Uh…" Victor stared up at her, hands out like he was preparing to catch her if need be. "What are you doing?"

"Signaling Greg," she told him, turning the flashlight app on and pointing it up.

Covering the light and then exposing it again, she repeated the signal several times until she noticed one of the flying creatures deviate from their loop.

Satisfied, Wendy hopped down with a solid *thud*, startling Victor.

"Geez, you're going to hurt yourself," he muttered. Following her to the next cross street, he asked, "What did you tell him?"

"To meet at home base, which this time would be the motel."

"What about Lady Moth? Where's she going to go?"

Wendy shook her head. "I don't know."

Fire trucks blazed past them, sirens wailing.

Victor hurried to keep up. "Shouldn't we try to—"

"I can't really think about that right now, Vic," she said, ignoring the ringing in her ears.

Just as she glanced over her shoulder, she spotted several police cars pulling up behind the fire engines.

A thunderous sound from inside the Mellon Center brought them to a halt, ducking and covering their heads on instinct.

Panic enveloped the mass of people as everyone rushed to get away from the building.

No fire, no crumbling structures…

A cloud of dust escaped the open front doors and faded into the gaps between people still trying to put distance between themselves and whatever was happening behind the steel and glass walls.

Victor pulled Wendy closer as he backed up towards another brick building, searching for a safe place to wait.

He swallowed. "Was that…"

Wendy gripped his forearm tightly. "I think that was the elevators."

A large shadow above them caught her attention and she glanced up.

Greg was soaring over the other skyscrapers, away from the chaos.

"We have to go," Wendy said, tugging on Victor's sleeve. "Now."

Keeping away from main streets, they rushed back to their car with hardly another word.

Just as Victor took the keys from her, Wendy exhaled roughly.

"Greg saved those people, didn't he?"

Nodding, Victor squeezed the tips of her fingers. "Yeah, he did."

* * * * * * *

Flicking the bathroom light off, Wendy stepped into the main room to see Victor standing in front of the TV with his arms folded and remote clenched in his hand.

"Please tell me we weren't wrong," she said. "Did something else…"

"No, no, we're good. We're really good." Victor turned to smile at her. "Watch."

Standing next to him, she stared at the live news update on the local station. He turned the volume up as Wendy read the scrolling feed at the bottom of the screen.

"…Authorities say a fire alarm was manually set off moments before one of the main elevators malfunctioned in BNY Mellon Center this afternoon…"

The talking head news reporter brushed her hair off her shoulder as she gestured behind her to the building being taped off by police officers.

"…An employee we spoke with said there was a commotion outside as two unidentified flying creatures were spotted attacking the skyscraper just before the alarm went off, causing some to speculate there was a correlation, however Police Sergeant Ruiz could not confirm that with us at this time…"

Wendy swallowed. "So many people saw Greg and the Lady Moth… There's no way the news station doesn't have footage."

"Maybe, but they're not showing it, and that's a small win, right?"

"I guess." Turning towards him, she murmured, "What if someone still got hurt, Vic? How do I tell Greg it was all for nothing?"

"Wait," he told her, gesturing to the T.V. again. "Look."

Focusing on the reporter still relaying details, Wendy took a deep breath.

"…were told that the elevators were still within safety standards after the case against Leopold Construction was settled last month, however a building inspector for the city has said that their criteria will be altered after today's incident. Thankfully, no one was injured by the elevator malfunction, despite the severity of the collapse. In fact, most employees were already outside by that time. This is still a developing story, but for now I think we can all agree a true tragedy was avoided today. Back to you at the station, Bob."

The knot in Wendy's chest loosened.

"See?" Victor said. "We did it. And Greg did it. Team effort on all fronts, but we—"

Wendy cut him off by wrapping her arms around his neck in a tight hug.

"Wha—Oh," he sputtered, laughing. "Okay, yeah, celebration hug."

"I can't believe that worked," she said, squeezing him harder.

Victor wrapped an arm around her waist. "Crisis averted. People are fine. Everything's--"

Wendy's head snapped up, staring him in the eyes. "Do you hear that?"

"You've got to stop saying that, my anxiety spikes every time."

"No, that clicking," she said, disengaging from the hug. "It sounds like it's coming from the bathroom."

Quietly, she opened the door and turned the light back on, waiting to hear the noise again.

By the small, opaque glass window next to the shower, she heard a short chirp.

"Greg?" Wendy stood on her tiptoes, pushing on the window to peer outside.

Crouched in the brush, two red eyes blinked up at her. *"I didn't know if I should use the door."*

Wendy beamed. "Oh my God, you're back."

"Of course," he clicked. *"You told me to meet at home base."*

"Think you can fit through this?" She asked, pointing to the windowsill.

"I can try."

He almost made it, but his wings jammed in the tight corners. After a hearty tug, Greg tumbled into the bathroom with a high-pitched screech, taking Wendy down with him.

"Oof, that looked painful," Victor said, hurrying to help them both up. As Greg stood, he brushed him off and playfully jiggled his wing. "You okay?"

Greg chirped and nodded in thanks.

The three of them stared in momentary silence.

"So… That was a hell of a day, huh?" Victor said, patting Greg's arm. "You want pizza for dinner? Extra barbeque sauce?"

Greg smiled, tiny fang teeth catching the light.

"Yup, thought so."

* * * * * * *

"Oh my God, that's so dorky!"

Wendy chucked her pizza crust at Victor and laughed. "It is not."

"You would stay up late to watch livestreams of the Nobel Prize ceremonies?" Victor wiped his mouth with a paper napkin. "Sorry but that's even nerdier than I imagined."

Greg wheezed out a chuckle as he scarfed down two slices of pineapple pizza smothered in barbeque sauce. *"It really is."*

Making an offended noise at the back of her throat, Wendy shook her head. "It's not like I was watching CSPAN all day."

"No, it might be worse."

"Fine, mock all you want, Valentine," she said, kicking Victor's chair leg just as he tilted back. "What's your big secret?"

Regaining his balance, he said, "I have no secrets, I'm an open book."

Greg shot a glance at Wendy, arching a dark eyebrow. "Oh yeah?"

Victor took a huge bite of his slice of pepperoni and nodded. "Mhm hm."

After considering it a moment, she grinned. "Okay, then tell us your most embarrassing…"

She looked over, seeing Greg pantomiming something from behind Victor. It looked like either a sign for choking or kissing, she couldn't tell.

Wendy shook her head. "Most embarrassing prom story."

"That would be junior prom," Victor announced, unfazed. "I ate some bad sweet and sour chicken right before picking up my date and got sick on the dance floor."

Wendy wrinkled her nose. "Ew, gross."

"You asked." Pivoting in his chair, Victor added, "What about you Greg? Any mortifying anecdotes you like to share?"

Greg chewed thoughtfully for a beat before grunting. *"I guess being made into an anatomically incorrect statue is pretty mortifying."*

Facing Wendy, Victor waited for her to translate.

"Oh yeah, the statue," he exclaimed. "You're right, it looks nothing like you."

"Especially the butt."

Wendy choked on her pizza.

"It's true."

Leaning over to change the music on Wendy's phone, Victor grinned. "Oh my God, you really are old," he said. "Aren't The Contours from the fifties?"

"They were used in *Dirty Dancing*," she argued. "I'm not a grandma."

"Your use of *Dirty Dancing* as evidence that you're not an old lady in a mask a-la *Scooby Doo* is actually proving my point."

"Shut up," she said, kicking his chair again. "Greg, you remember this right?"

Nodding, Greg closed his eyes, bopping his head from side to side.

"Remember our choreography?"

Greg's eyes opened wide as he chirped.

Tossing his pizza box to the side, he hopped up and folded his wings tight against his back to keep from knocking anything over. Giggling, Wendy stood and spun, stepping in line with Greg as they hummed the words to "Do You Love Me".

They were a little rusty, but soon they were on the beat, doing their own version of the twist. Squatting down low, they wiggled their hips as they moved back and forth. Greg's shoulder shimmy was infinitely better than Wendy's, but she had the foot placements down pat.

"Okay, I take it back," Victor said, smiling at Wendy. "No grandma could do that without busting a knee."

"Told you."

Setting his pizza down, Victor launched himself out of his chair. "Alright, I'm feeling left out," he said. Pointing to Greg, he asked, "You know how to moon walk?"

Greg furrowed his brow and shook his head.

"Great, then I'm going to teach you."

Surprisingly, Greg was a natural.

Victor however nearly broke the lamp. Twice.

Chapter Eighteen

Rolling over to the edge of the bed, Wendy squinted down at the floor.

"Greg? You awake?"

"Yep," he clicked softly. *"And hungry."*

She breathed out a laugh. "You're always hungry."

"Are there any Twinkies left?"

"Probably."

"Excellent."

Before he could sit up to go rummaging around, Wendy reached for him. "Hey, I didn't get to talk to you earlier…"

Leaning onto his elbow, Greg stared up at her. *"About what?"*

"About… Everything." She inhaled. "What I did at the Mellon Center. Outing you to all those people. I didn't…" She shook her head. "I didn't know what else do to."

A large, calloused hand took hers. *"I know,"* he chirped. *"You did exactly what we were trying to do: Get everyone's attention."*

Wendy frowned. "I know, but it didn't feel good. I should be protecting you, not tossing you to the social media wolves. I mean, God, all the videos taken today…"

Red, reflective eyes softened as he gazed up. *"You don't have to protect me all the time,"* he clicked. *"I'm tougher than I look."*

Wendy laughed, and covered her mouth. "I guess you're right."

"Hey, Wendy?" Even in the dark, she could see the concern on Greg's face.

"Yeah?"

"I'm nervous about tomorrow."

They'd narrowed down the closest possible wooded areas. Wendy had suggested they start near water and move out from there. Greg would be able to hear the others before she or Victor could and know which direction to head.

It would be a long day, and there was still a possibility they might not find anything, but if everything went according to plan…

Greg would finally be reuniting with other Mothmen.

"Me too," she admitted. "But you said the Lady Moth was nice, right?"

Greg hummed and nodded. *"She said there are others. Lots of others. I… I don't remember there being that many."*

"To be fair, you don't remember a whole lot before nineteen sixty-seven."

He chuckled. *"True."*

From the other bed, Victor grunted and flopped over. "Is it time for school, mom?"

Wendy and Greg paused, staring at each other in the dark before laughing quietly.

"I'm going to miss you," she blurted out, squeezing Greg's talon.

Sadness filled the space between them, drawing the night in closer.

"Maybe I won't stay," Greg eventually clicked. *"You said yourself I don't have to. West Virginia is home."*

Tears pricked Wendy's eyes and she blinked them away. "Right. You don't have to stay. But you might want to. Even for just a little while."

Greg shrugged one shoulder, growing quiet once more.

"First we have to find them," she said, trying to lighten the mood. "And if Victor is as slow tomorrow as he was walking to your bunker, that might never happen."

Grinning, he turned his head to look at Victor who had started snoring. *"I'm glad you have someone."*

"What do you mean?"

Arching an eyebrow at her, Greg stared for a moment. *"You know what I mean. You found someone who makes things… easier. Better."*

Glancing over at the shape of Victor sprawled awkwardly across his bed, Wendy tilted her head. "Yeah, I guess…"

"I'm glad you have him. Even if he is a terrible dancer."

Patting Greg's hand, she smiled. "Don't worry. You're still my favorite dance partner."

* * * * * * *

October 1st, 2016

Keeping a death grip on her red plastic cup, Wendy maneuvered slowly through the crowded dorm suite.

She didn't want to be there. She'd been perfectly content watching Netflix in her pajamas. But her roommate Clara had made the first few weeks of freshman year much more bearable than she'd ever imagined, so when she asked her to go with her to the party across campus, Wendy couldn't find it in her to say no.

That didn't mean she had to dive into the kegger stereotype head first though.

Narrowly avoiding a collision with a tipsy jock type, she Bee-lined for the corner of the room that seemed less populated.

She quickly understood why.

The card table stacked with board games didn't seem to be of interest to anyone.

Sipping from her foamy beer, Wendy glanced around, keeping a look out for Clara on her way back from the snack table.

At first, she thought the guy in red plaid was waving at someone else.

Then she realized she was the only one in that particular corner, so unless he was enthusiastically greeting the Inception poster behind her...

"Hey," he called from his perch on the thrift store couch arm. "You're in my chem lab, right? Uh, Wendy?"

She nodded. "Yeah. And you're... Vince?"

"Victor."

Wendy grimaced. Great start making friends already.

"Sorry," she said.

Swinging his leg over, Victor stood up. "Nah, it's okay. You were close though, so ten points to Gryffindor."

"Ha, thanks," she said into her cup. "I love those books."

His eyes lit up. "Me too! Which is your favorite?"

Taking half a step forward, she said, "The fourth. You?"

"The third, but I think that's just 'cause I wanted to be Sirius Black."

"Well, who could blame you," she said, chuckling softly.

Maybe she could do this. Maybe she could make friends in a new town, in a new state, and not have a total socially anxious break down.

Swirling the half of her beer left around in her cup, she glanced up. "Are you a freshman too?"

Victor shook his head. "Sophomore. Wait, you're a freshman?"

Oh no. She'd blown it already.

"Yeah... Why? Is that bad?"

He smiled. "No, not at all. You're just not diving into the Bacchanalia like the other freshies."

"Forbidden fruit was never really a thing for me. My mom would share her wine coolers with me, and my dad let me have a beer once in a while on holidays."

Tucking his hand into his front pocket, he looked around the room. "So this is old hat for you then, huh?"

"This, isn't," she said, gesturing to the mob of people in the middle of the room attempting some sort of drinking game. "This is..."

"Overwhelming?"

The tension between her shoulder blades ebbed. "Very much so."

Setting his drink down on the game table, Victor inspected the window for a moment before turning around. "Ever been on the roof?"

That tension returned tenfold.

"Um, no," *she said, scowling.*

"Did you want to see? It's way quieter and the view's pretty nice."

Wendy froze. This was the beginning of a Law and Order episode, she just knew it.

"You're not going to sexually assault me and throw me off, are you?"

Victor blinked owlishly at her. "God, no. I was just going to show you the theater majors doing improv on the quad." *He backed up a fraction.* "But, yeah, I could see how inviting a girl onto the roof would look incredibly dubious for multiple reasons, and I'm now imagining my mom scolding me for the next three years, so..."

Wendy laughed, nearly spilling her beer. "It's okay. The safety seminar was just really intense."

"I heard a rumor they passed out tasers this year."

"No, but pepper spray was heavily endorsed."

"Good for them." *Smiling, he twisted the lock on the window and slid it open.* "You want me to go first or...?"

Taking one last swallow of her drink, Wendy set the cup down and started crawling out onto the fire escape.

"Alright, looks like you're a pretty confident climber then," he said, following her out.

Victor had been right. The view was nice. And the cringe-worthy improv was just terrible enough to be entertaining.

But Wendy found herself enjoying Victor's company more.

He was sweet, and funny, and he didn't balk at her ambitious college career plans.

She was suddenly very grateful to Clara for making her go to that party.

"Okay, so, I kind of have something to tell you," he said, swinging one leg over the ledge they'd camped out on. "Most people laugh, but it's my litmus test for new friends."

Curious, Wendy stayed quiet, waiting for him to continue.

"You've heard of Big Foot, right?"

A frown etched itself deep into her forehead. "Yes?"

"And the Loch Ness Monster?"

"This is some litmus test."

Victor chuckled. "I know, I know, but... See, the thing is, I actually really believe in them. Cryptids. Sasquatch, Beast of Bray Road, Mothman..."

Wendy tried very hard not to have a visible reaction to the mention of Greg.

By the way Victor continued listing creatures without missing a beat, she figured she was successful.

"I want to study them some day," Victor continued. "But not in an awful, government agency in E.T. way. I just want to learn about them and get them recognized as endangered species."

The urge to fidget was too strong for Wendy to fight. She plucked at the seam of her jeans just below the knee as she listened.

"I know it's weird," he said. "And not everyone believes, which is fine, but I like to tell people ahead of time so they're not caught off guard by how many books on Chupacabra I own."

Steadying herself, Wendy looked up from the thread she was slowly working free from the denim along her calf.

*"Well, I don't exactly believe..." The lie felt strange rolling around in her mouth. "But it doesn't bother me how much **you** do."*

Victor's smile widened.

"Did I pass?" She asked.

Feigning disinterest, he sniffed and jerked his chin up. "The preliminary, at least. We'll see how you do further into the quarter."

"I guess I better start studying then," she said with a smirk.

Wendy left that night with a new friend, and a plan to buy Clara apology bagels for ditching her at the party. She didn't seem to mind too much though, if the two phone numbers she got were any indication.

* * * * * * *

The drive to Raccoon Creek State Park was long.

Well, it felt long at six o'clock in the morning.

"Careful with chugging that," Victor said, nodding to her large coffee. "You'll make yourself sick."

"And I'll die if I have to continue being conscious without more caffeine in my system."

He smirked, shaking his head. "So dramatic."

"Can I take this off now?" Greg grunted from under the blanket.

"Sure, big guy," Victor said, and then turned to beam at them both. "Oh my God, I got that. I'm learning Greg-speak!"

"A true feat. Now please watch the road," Wendy said from behind the paper cup.

Unaffected, Victor responded, "You're so grumpy today."

"Sorry, I didn't get a lot of sleep."

"Yeah, speaking of, were you two eating Twinkies at two a.m. or did I dream that?"

Glancing over her shoulder, Wendy smiled. "Definitely a dream."

"What if the others don't like Twinkies?" Greg asked, suddenly aghast.

"Guess you'll have to proselytize to them about the glory of snack cakes," Wendy said.

Making a turn, Victor checked the GPS on his phone.

"Alright, this looks like the parking area…" He slowed the car as he bent to look out the windshield. "This looks pretty populated. Do we really think Moth-kin would live around here?"

Gulping the remnants of her coffee, Wendy glanced out the window. "Point Pleasant isn't exactly a ghost town. If they could find a secluded spot with trees big enough to hide in, I'm sure they'd be fine."

Pulling as close as he could to one of the trail entrances, Victor kept watch as Wendy and Greg hopped out and ran for cover in the brush.

"I'll be two minutes," he called as he backed up and turned, searching for a parking space.

Out of necessity, they had to stay off the path, but Wendy was happy to rough it through the woods. Years of wandering through miles upon miles of forest in the

McClintic reserve had prepared her for any kind of terrain off the trails.

And if she were being honest, it was more fun that way. Like being a kid again.

Victor wasn't having nearly as an enjoyable time, however.

"I should have doubled up on the bug spray," he said, slapping the side of his neck, squashing a mosquito. "Ew, God, that one was massive. Like Count Dracula."

"I told you," Wendy laughed, jumping from rock to rock along a mossy stretch. "Hey, be careful you don't—"

Victor slipped in a patch of mud, feet going completely out from under him, and landed flat on his back with a low groan.

"...Fall," Wendy finished with a wince.

Sitting up slowly, he rubbed the back of his head. "I'm alright."

Greg's wheezing laugh could be heard from the trees above them.

"Hey, don't kick a guy while he's literally down," Victor called up to the shaking branch.

Hopping off the large rock she'd balanced on, Wendy went over, offering a hand.

"Maybe you've got a career in slap-stick," she said, helping him to his feet.

"A-ha, very funny," he said, attempting to wipe the dirt from his jeans and failing. "Greg, are we getting any closer? My noodle legs are getting tired."

Gliding to another tree, Greg perched himself and cocked his head.

After a moment, he clicked, *"I hear water... Maybe they'll be close by?"*

As Wendy translated, Victor sighed.

"Maybe, huh?"

Patting him on the shoulder, Wendy smiled. "Just think of all the other Moth-kin you'll get to meet once we're there."

"I know you're teasing me but that is actually a good motivator." Dusting his hands off, Victor looked up. "Alright, which way Greg?"

They continued to hike at a steady pace, weaving their way through the trees and tall grasses, over fallen logs and rocks, towards the sound of a babbling creek. Greg glided down from the treetops, lumbering on all fours at Wendy's side.

They both pretended not to notice Victor typing notes on his phone as they walked.

"There," Wendy said, pointing through the thinning tree line.

The water glittered in the midmorning sun as it flowed around the bend.

Stopping at the bank, Victor planted his hands on his hips and tried to catch his breath.

"Pretty," he said, panting. "And Moth-kin-less. Greg? Any directional advice?"

Sitting back on his heels, Greg tilted his left ear towards the sky. *"Across the water, into the woods a bit. I think I hear them."*

Victor paled once Wendy interpreted. "*Across* the water?"

"C'mon," she said, smirking as she shook her head. "I'll keep you from drowning."

"I'd appreciate that," he said, following her.

Thankfully, before Victor had to try his luck doggie paddling, they found a wooden foot bridge several meters down river.

Wendy brought up the rear and tried not to laugh as Victor practically skipped across in gleeful relief.

Heavily wooded hills began to flatten into a narrow valley, and at Greg's behest, they followed the curve, pausing a few times for him to listen.

As soon as they lost sight of the water, she could feel a shift.

Goosepimples dotted her arms and lower legs despite the Spring warmth, and the hair on the back of her neck stood on end. Her knees turned spongy as she walked.

She didn't know how, but she could sense it.

They were close.

"Vic," she whispered, reaching for him. "I think they're here."

He stopped, looking from her to the woods around them. "Watching us?"

"I don't know. But I think they're close by."

Passing them, Greg continued on, pulled forward by conviction and instinct.

The valley widened, revealing a small hill covered in wildflowers and clover. The hum of bumble bees was a baritone note to the twittering of songbirds in the nearby branches.

"Greg?" Wendy called.

The urgency building in her chest was echoed in his hurried shuffle across the expanse of grass. They were entering liminal territory—not quite otherworldly, but certainly no where close to being mundane.

They'd found them.

Cresting over the hilltop, Wendy and Victor halted in astonishment.

Dark figures dotted the sun-drenched meadow, crouching with wings folded over their shoulders. They'd all stilled, listening and waiting for the approach of two strangers and one lost beloved. Each one tilted their head, watching in curiosity.

Greg stopped, peering over the blades of the tall grass timidly.

A smaller Moth-kin inched forward, blinking wide reddish-brown eyes at him before clicking softly.

"Is that… Lady Moth?" Victor asked, unable to tear his gaze away from the group.

Wendy could only nod.

Her breath hitched as she took in the small clan of Mothmen.

Greg chirped a greeting, hoping for their welcome.

It came in a chorus of gleeful clicks and squeaks before all the Moth-kin rushed forward. A larger Mothman, much lighter in their coloring, reached for Greg, clutching his arms and then the back of his head, pressing their foreheads together as they trilled.

"What's going on?" Victor asked, barely above a whisper.

Tears spilled down Wendy's cheeks as she watched.

"They're welcoming him home," she murmured. Sniffing, she wiped her face. "They missed him. They missed him so much."

Completely encircled in Moth-kin, Greg turned, greeting everyone with joyful chatter.

When there was a break in the group, he sat up taller to see Wendy and Victor, and gestured to them.

"These are my friends," he clicked. *"They helped me find you."*

All five Mothmen faced them and chirped. *"Welcome Greg-friends!"*

Victor's delighted laugh bubbled out of his chest.

Pumping his fist, he exclaimed, "This is officially the best day *ever*."

* * * * * * *

"Tag! You're it!"

Victor spun around in the middle of the field. "Hey, that's not fair. You have wings."

Gurgling laughter rolled through the air as the two juvenile Moth-kin hopped and glided over his head.

"Come back here," he called, chasing after them.

Smiling as she watched, Wendy leaned back on her hands, settling into the soft grass.

The dewy morning had burned off into a pleasant, warm midday without a cloud in sight.

So, naturally, when the youngest of the Mothmen—the age equivalent of children, Wendy guessed—introduced themselves, the next question out of their mouths was, did they want to play a game.

Victor had nearly shoved Wendy over in his enthusiasm.

She'd decided to sit that round out. Let him have his moment.

Besides, she couldn't say no to the chance to speak with the elders of the Moth-clan.

Meeting the parents was always important.

The charcoal grey one glanced from her to Victor and then to Greg. *"They both saved you?"*

Greg chirped. *"Victor is a new friend. But Wendy did."*

She blinked, furrowing her brow. "I didn't save you, Greg," she murmured. "You saved *me* that day."

His gaze softened. *"No, Wendy. You saved me."*

Before she could ask him what he meant, Lady Moth hopped over to join their semicircle.

"We thought you were no longer," she clicked. *"Seeing you that night... I couldn't wait to tell them you'd returned."*

Shifting his weight on his haunches, Greg looked around the group. *"Do... Do you know who I was? Before I fell?"*

Confusion rippled through the others as they shared uncertain stares.

"You were us," one of the others chirped quietly. *"You were family. You still are."*

"Did Greg have a job all those years ago?" Wendy asked. "Before he lost his memory?"

Lady Moth grinned, flashing her tiny fang-like teeth. *"Same as all of us. To protect what's here."*

Warmth spread through Wendy's chest. She'd been right.

Greg wasn't a monster or a devil or a threat.

He was a guardian.

"So, why did you all leave West Virginia?"

The other Moth-kin looked to one another, perplexed.

"We were never there. He went on his own."

Greg's head snapped up. *"I did?"*

The older charcoal colored one nodded. *"You said you could feel a pull... That something there needed you."*

"When was this?" Wendy asked, leaning forward.

"Many, many years ago." The other Mothman patted Greg's shoulder with a large hand. *"You were much younger then."*

"You would come back to see us," one said. *"Tell us about the new place you'd claimed. The people there. The forest and the animals. But then... You stopped returning."*

"I fell," Greg explained. *"I only remember waking up in the woods and stumbling out into the road. I came across a group in a car and tried to talk to them."* He chuckled low in his throat. *"I only managed to scare them."*

Lady Moth turned to Wendy, covering her hand with large talons. *"You didn't scare this one though."*

Before she could tell them she had, in fact, been very afraid of Greg at first, he spoke.

"No. Wendy doesn't scare easily."

A commotion in the middle of the meadow brought their heads around just in time to see Victor attempting to catch one of the child Moth-kin by their foot.

Apparently, he'd lost his shoe during their game, and it had become an object of much interest to the two younglings.

The elder Mothmen clicked in unison. *"Put that back where it belongs."*

With a pathetic groan, the one holding the sneaker glided back to the ground.

But instead of simply handing the shoe to Victor, they dropped onto all fours and nearly upended him to put it back on his foot themselves.

"Wha—Whoa, wait," Victor cried, flapping his arms for balance.

"Hold still please, your feet coverings are strange," the young Moth-kin chirped, holding onto Victor's ankle.

"Uh, Wendy? Maybe some help here?"

She tried so hard not to laugh.

At least, that's what she told herself.

Covering her mouth, Wendy doubled over, giggling uncontrollably.

Victor lost his battle and landed on his backside with a loud *thunk*.

"That's better," the kid Moth chirped, wriggling the shoe over his toes.

The two elders glanced at one another and smiled.

"They'll never be this entertained again," one clicked.

Wendy caught her breath and nodded. "Victor has a way of making everything an adventure."

She blatantly ignored the cheesy grin on Greg's face as he stared at her.

Lady Moth focused her reddish-brown eyes on Wendy. *"Will you stay a while? There's so much to talk about."*

Smiling, Wendy jerked her chin. "Yes. I'd love that."

* * * * * * *

Greg held up the plastic wrapper, gesturing with one talon. *"This is a Twinkie,"* he explained. *"And this…"* He picked up the bottle next to him. *"Is barbeque sauce. Together, they're delicious. A true delicacy."*

The other Moth-kin clicked in fascination.

"Here, try one," Greg chirped, passing the snack cakes out.

From behind her, Wendy could hear Victor trying not to gag. Turning to shush him, she stopped at the sight of the two young Mothmen squatting with Victor seated between them, combing through his hair with their claws as if grooming him.

"Um, Vic?"

He looked up at her. "Don't ask. They just sat me down and started doing this," he said, gesturing to his head. "I hope this doesn't mean I have lice."

The one at his back glanced over and shook their head. *"His hair is just so different. And kind of… greasy."*

Wendy snorted. "Most human males are."

"Huh?"

"Nothing."

Facing the rest of the group again, she watched as Greg shared his favorite things, explaining the various snacks he'd brought and the CD player. He helped Lady Moth with the ear buds and turned it on, making her screech in surprise.

"Sorry, I forgot to turn the volume down."

After a moment, she looked up, eyes wide and glittering. *"I... I like this,"* she clicked.

Wendy had imagined this reunion a million different ways, but hadn't expected most of it would be spent sharing junk food and explaining modern country music.

It was... A very Greg thing to do.

One of the elder Mothmen shuffled closer to her, reaching for her hand. *"Thank you, Wendy-friend,"* they chirped quietly. *"For bringing him back to us."*

Swallowing passed the sudden lump in her throat, Wendy said, "Greg is my best friend in the whole world. I would do anything for him."

"He told us about your town," they clicked. *"The Point Pleasant that celebrates our kind."*

Wendy smiled. "Greg's kind of a celebrity there."

"Perhaps, one day, we can all see this place."

"I'd love that." She inhaled, steadying herself. "It would be great to see you all again."

"I know he's just come back, but I can't help but expect him to go away once more."

Wendy's brows drew together. "What do you mean?"

"Greg has two worlds now," they explained. *"It would be unfair to make him choose."*

"That's true," she started, voice dropping. "But I know how lonely he's been. And as much as my town loves him, it isn't the same as having a family to surround him."

Victor's yelp caught their attention, making them turn.

"Ow, ow, my scalp is still attached to that, you know," he said, neck arched from where the young Moth-kin had yanked his head back by the hair.

The elder hissed, chastising them for abusing their guest.

Both younglings immediately started petting Victor, soothing him with gentle strokes of their talons.

"Sorry, Victor-friend," they chirped.

He laughed as one rubbed their entire palm down his face. "It's okay. Hey, do you two want to learn how to moon walk?"

* * * * * * *

The sun dipped lower in the sky, filtering a golden light through the leaves across the meadow.

Afternoon was quickly fading into dusk, and with every passing moment, the gnawing in Wendy's stomach intensified.

They'd have to leave soon.

And she already knew what Greg's decision would be.

Human footsteps approached on her right, but Wendy kept her gaze on the trio of Mothmen several yards away.

"Do you think there's a market for a Moth-kid babysitter," Victor said, plopping down on the grass next to her. "'Cause if so, I'm going to corner the market. I might not be as strong as them, but I can hold my own, and I've clearly got the energy to chase after them so…"

Wendy attempted a watery smile, but it quickly dissolved into a sorrowful grimace.

"Hey," Victor murmured, reaching for her. "I can't really imagine what you're feeling right now, but you did a great thing by helping Greg find his family."

Sniffing back tears, she nodded and stared at a patch of clover in front of her. "I'm happy for him," she said. "I am. But I'm also…"

"Devastated?"

"Yeah." Wendy glanced up. "Does that make me a terrible friend?"

Victor squeezed her wrist gently. "No. It makes you human." Looking over at the Moth-kin nearby, he tilted his head. "It makes you a living being. With a broad spectrum of emotion and the capacity to contain multitudes."

She wasn't sure if Victor had always been that wise or if it was a new development, but either way, Wendy was grateful to have him with her in that moment.

"Thanks, Vic," she said, lips curving.

Then she blinked, registering a distinct change in his appearance.

"Wait, where's your plaid shirt?"

"Oh, one of the kiddie Moths really liked the buttons, so I let them have it," he said, jerking his thumb over his shoulder. "It's fine, I have four just like it at home."

Wendy smiled. "I think you'd make a really great Mothman nanny."

"I'm definitely putting that down on my resumé." Shading his eyes, Victor looked up at the vibrant sunset. "So, I don't mean to rush this, but it's getting late. And if you thought I was a klutz in the daytime, you don't want to see me try to hike at night."

Grief soured her stomach, but Wendy nodded anyway.

"You're right," she said. "We should go."

Standing up, Victor offered her a hand and pulled her to her feet.

As soon as the moved, the Mothmen sensed their impending departure, and hurried to encircle them.

"Please don't go yet, Greg-friends—"

"When will we see you again?"

"Are you sure you don't want to stay longer?"

"Wendy-friend, can we play with your hair next?"

Through the tears threatening to fall, she laughed. "This is worse than my family reunions."

Breaking away from the group, Greg stood and led Wendy by the hand to the side.

It was easy to forget how giant he was when he was crouched on all fours or flying over treetops. But there in the meadow, Greg's broad frame and impossible height blocked the setting sun, casting her in shadow.

Wendy savored it.

"I told you you'd like them," she said, trying to smile bravely.

Greg saw through it immediately.

"I don't want you to be sad, Wendy."

She exhaled slowly. "I'm not. Not really."

He arched an eyebrow at her, and she relented.

"Okay, yes, I am sad. But not because of this," she said, gesturing to the Moth-kin who were still saying farewell to Victor. "I'm so glad you have your family, Greg."

"I always had my family," he chirped. *"Now I just have more."*

Wendy glanced over at the others. "They said you told them about Point Pleasant. I think they'd like to come visit sometime."

Nodding vigorously, Greg opened his mouth, but Wendy cut him off.

"Just promise me something, okay?" She waited for him to click in agreement before continuing. "Don't come back too soon."

He furrowed his dark brows in confusion, staring down at her in silence.

"If you come back too soon, you'll be cheating yourself out of time with your family. I know you, I know you'll want to stay in West Virginia, but they've been missing you for over fifty years. We've had our time with you, Greg. This is your chance to have time with them now."

"But... I'll miss you."

Hot tears rolled down Wendy's cheeks.

"I'll miss you too," she whispered.

Pulling her forward by the hands, Greg wrapped his arms around her in a bear hug.

"I don't know how long I'll manage out here," he grunted softly. *"They don't even know who Taylor Swift is."*

Wendy sputtered a laugh into Greg's fuzzy torso. "And you'll run out of Twinkies eventually."

"Oh no, I didn't think about the Twinkies."

"Just more incentive to see me eventually," she said, digging her fingers into his back.

Stroking her hair, Greg clicked, *"I don't need incentive to see my best friend."*

Fresh tears fell from her lashes, matting the velveteen fur pressed against her cheek.

"Please be safe," she said. "And try not to be seen by too many people. And if those Paranormal Explorer guys come around—"

"I know, I know," he chirped. *"I'll hide."*

"Good."

Holding onto him tighter, one last time, Wendy tried to gather her strength.

"I miss you already," she said.

"Me too."

Ever so slowly, Greg released her from the hug and dropped down into a crouch in front of her.

Just like he had the day they met.

"Goodbye, Wendy."

"Not bye," she told him, taking his hand in hers. "Just later."

Chapter Nineteen

The student union buzzed with the kind of terrified panic only end of semester finals could conjure.

It was the modern equivalent of a biblical plague, only instead of being passed over, everyone just hoped they passed.

A heavy stack of books dropped onto the table next to Wendy, and she cursed under her breath, glaring at the highlighter smudge on her notes.

"Gee, thanks so much for that," she said, rubbing at the yellow with her thumb to no avail.

Glaring up at the offending person, ready to tell them to find another study buddy to harass, she stopped at the sight of Victor beaming down at her.

"What are you doing here? And what are you doing with all these history books?"

Pulling out a seat, he plopped himself down as gracefully as he had his reading material.

"I have some news, and I think you're going to be pretty excited about it."

"I already told you, discovering a new flavor of Pop-Tarts is not news."

"Okay, one, you're wrong. And two, this isn't about Pop-Tarts."

Sighing, Wendy capped her highlighter and set it aside. "Victor, I am neck deep in studying for finals, and I still have the rest of my term paper to write, so unless this is life altering, earth shattering—"

Unfolding a piece of paper, Victor held it up in front of her face. "Read."

Wendy took it from him and rolled her eyes. "Fine."

After scanning the first few lines, she straightened in her seat.

She couldn't have read that right…

"Wait, what?"

"You are looking at the very first Crypto-folkloric anthropology major in the history of Ohio State University." Victor grinned so broadly his face threatened to split in half.

"You…"

"Convinced Doctor Bledsoe that while, perhaps in her mind, we can't study cryptids as we would any other culture, we can study their impact on our culture via folklore and history. And after some considerable groveling and self-flagellation as well as promising never to ask her for another favor for the rest of my college career, she said yes." He flung out his arms in celebration. "Can you believe it?"

"I… actually can," she said, rereading Doctor Bledsoe's signature on the form and smiling. "So, wait, what are all these then?" She pointed to the pile of books in front of them.

"Oh, that's for my catch-up work," he said. "Apparently when you create a major that involves blending two separate ones, the workload doubles. But my spirits will not be deadened. This is a House Valentine victory."

Wendy started to fold the paper back and hand it to him when her gaze landed on a name she recognized, and she did a double take.

"Hold on," she said, examining the final line once more. "This says you'll be showing real-world applications of this major at your new internship… At the Mothman Museum?" She glanced up. "In Point Pleasant?"

Victor's cheeks flushed as he scratched the back of his neck.

"Uh, yeah, I meant to tell you about that…" Settling into his chair, he continued. "I wanted to show Doctor Bledsoe there are already people out there collecting information about cryptids for historical research and decided maybe if I could come to the board with an internship already lined up, they'd be more amenable."

Wendy blinked. "You're going to be working in Point Pleasant?"

"Only a few days a week, but yeah," he said. "It's not that far of a drive."

"It's at least an hour from your place. One way."

"So, I'll download a bunch of podcasts to listen to on the commute," he said, smiling. "It'll be worth the spent gas."

Tapping the edge of the table, his gaze darted from her to the paper still in her hands and then back again.

"And, you know, I was thinking… Since you'll be back home over the summer, and I'll be in town, if you're free, maybe we could—"

Wendy couldn't wait any longer.

Tossing the paper onto her notebook, she shot forward, nearly falling out of her chair as she grabbed him by the front of his X-Men tee shirt. Hauling him close, she crushed her mouth to his a little more forcefully than she'd intended but the affect was all the same.

Too stunned to move, Victor blinked rapidly, lashes brushing the curves of her cheeks with each flutter.

Just as she was about to ease back, two incredibly warm hands cupped her face, angling her back just enough to deepen the kiss.

So *that's* what all the love songs were talking about…

Wendy sighed against him as goosebumps spread over her arms, chills dancing all the way up her spine to the top of her head, making her scalp tingle.

Twisting her grip in his shirt, she held onto Victor like he was the last great thing on earth.

He was certainly in the top three.

Top two if he'd keep doing that light scratching thing at the base of her neck.

In need of air and a little equilibrium, they broke apart, staring at each other in baffled silence.

And then Wendy smiled.

"Wow," Victor breathed. "That was…"

"Too much?"

"Amazing," he said, a bright grin spreading across his face.

Inching closer, their knees knocked together but neither minded. Reaching up, Victor brushed her curls off her forehead before leaning in to kiss her once more.

"Yep, definitely amazing. Incredible. Better than I ever imagined," he rambled.

Arching an eyebrow, Wendy smirked. "Thought about it, huh?"

"Only… every other hour since the day we met." A pink hue flooded his cheeks as he laughed softly. "Pretty corny, right?"

Smoothing the wrinkles she'd created in his shirt, Wendy tilted her head. "Well, what's that saying about good things and waiting?"

Victor's smile was infectious. "Man, I hope that's not a question on your final, otherwise you're screwed."

Laughing, Wendy pushed him away with a palm to his cheek. "Dork."

Victor grabbed her hand, threading their fingers together. "Yeah, but I'm your dork now."

He *sure* was.

* * * * * * *

April 29th, 2008

Swinging her legs over either side of the fallen log, Wendy gazed down at the shallow creek, watching the tiny fish dart through the water.

"Wendy, I have a question."

Greg leapt into the air, gliding over the stream to land on the log next to her.

"Shoot," she said, looking up.

"It's a little silly."

Reaching into her overalls pocket, she retrieved two pieces of gum and unwrapped them.

"That's okay," she said, popping the first into her mouth. "You should hear some of the silly questions kids in my class ask the teacher."

Handing the other piece of gum to Greg, she waited for him to chew a few times before urging him to continue.

"Well... I've been thinking, and I... I was wondering what love is."

"Love?" She echoed.

"I've heard of it," *Greg clicked, smacking his Double Bubble.* **"But I wonder if it's different for people and... me."**

Kicking her feet, Wendy focused on the flap, flap, flap of her loose shoelace for a moment.

"I don't know if love is different for creatures like you," she said finally. "But... It's kind of like a big hug on your insides. It's like finding out you don't have to go to school 'cause it's a snow day. It's just liking something or someone so much you only want to see them, and talk to them, and you don't mind if they take the last chip left in the bag 'cause you probably would have given it to them anyway."

"That's love?"

Wendy shrugged. "I think so. It's what it seems like to me, anyway." After a moment of thought, she added, "I guess it's also like feeling safe, and warm, and comfortable. Like nothing can really bother you. Like... you're home."

"Huh," *Greg hummed, staring up at the leaves rustling in the breeze.*

"Yeah, grown ups make a big deal about love being hard or scary, but seems to me it would be the easiest thing in the world. Loving someone just makes things better."

As she practiced blowing a bubble, finally able to get it larger than a quarter, Greg sat next to her in silence.

After the third pop, he turned towards her.

"Can friends love each other?"

"Of course," she said, stretching her gum with her fingers. "Friends should love each other. It's what makes you want to hang around them so much."

Greg smiled at her, showing his rows of tiny sharp teeth.

"Then, I guess that means I love you," he chirped, ears wiggling in delight.

Stuffing her gum back in her mouth, Wendy beamed. "I love you too, Greg."

Hoisting one leg over the log and jumping down into the creek with a great splash, she waved for him to follow.

"C'mon Greg, let's go build a fort."

Clicking happily, he swooped down, and followed her deeper into the woods.

Epilogue

June 9th, 2026

Humming the melody to her dad's favorite Oasis song, Wendy slid open the door to the back deck and stepped outside.

Dusk lingered in deep pinks and indigo clouds, but nighttime felt even further away than usual.

It was only because she was excited. And eager.

Wendy wasn't the most patient of people, she'd admit.

Rocking the wiggly bundle in her arms, she continued to mumble the lyrics to "Champagne Supernova" as Mary stared up at her in fascination.

She always looked the most like Victor when she was intrigued by something new—today it was Wendy's silver drop earrings.

Shifting the newborn to a more comfortable position in the crook of her elbow, she strode over to the railing of the deck, staring out over the lawn and small grove of trees at the edge of their property.

The windchime hanging on a hook by the steps clinked softly in the breeze.

Pressing her nose into the corn silk wisps of hair on top of Mary's head, she breathed in and smiled.

"I have a secret to tell you," Wendy whispered to her daughter. "Your daddy is my best friend, but he wasn't my *first* best friend."

Mary cooed, pulling her arm free from the quilted blankets.

"I know, shocking. But it's true," she said, swaying and rocking. "And today, you get let in on an even bigger family secret. One you're going to have to take very seriously because if I'm right, you're going to have a new best friend too."

As the sky darkened to a plum violet, with only the faintest rays still offering some light, she saw the movement in the distance. To anyone else, it would have looked like a large bird—an owl, or a hawk—soaring over the trees.

But Wendy knew better.

As the figure grew closer, she heard the high-pitched chirping she'd recognize anywhere.

Smiling, she angled her arm to prop Mary up so she could see.

Huge wings flapped as he made his descent towards their modest home.

"Look, Mary," Wendy murmured, pointing into the sky. "There he is."

She waved and held her daughter's tiny hand between her fingers.

"There's our friend, Greg."

About the Author

Lauren Devora is a North Carolina native now living in the greater Boston area of Massachusetts with her two huge dogs and ever-expanding coffee mug collection.

A life-long lover of stories and the fantastical, this book is the culmination of both of those things as well as her adoration for cryptids and the unknown.

You can find out more about her or her other works on her website laurendevora.com.

Made in the USA
Middletown, DE
17 December 2020